W9-BXP-452

3650 Summit Boulevard
West Palm Beach, FL   33406-4198

MR KATŌ
PLAYS
FAMILY

BY MILENA MICHIKO FLAŠAR

I Called Him Necktie

Mr Katō Plays Family

MR KATŌ PLAYS FAMILY

MILENA MICHIKO FLAŠAR

Translated by Caroline Froh

FORGE

TOR PUBLISHING GROUP

NEW YORK

This is a work of fiction. All of the characters, organizations, and events portrayed in this novel are either products of the author's imagination or are used fictitiously.

MR KATŌ PLAYS FAMILY

Copyright © 2018 by Milena Michiko Flašar
English translation © 2023 by Caroline Froh

Originally published in Germany as *Herr Katō spielt Familie* by Verlag Klaus Wagenbach.

All rights reserved.

A Forge Book
Published by Tom Doherty Associates / Tor Publishing Group
120 Broadway
New York, NY 10271

www.tor-forge.com

Forge® is a registered trademark of Macmillan Publishing Group, LLC.

The Library of Congress Cataloging-in-Publication Data
is available upon request.

ISBN 978-1-250-84249-7 (hardcover)
ISBN 978-1-250-84248-0 (ebook)

Our books may be purchased in bulk for promotional, educational, or business use. Please contact your local bookseller or the Macmillan Corporate and Premium Sales Department at 1-800-221-7945, extension 5442, or by email at MacmillanSpecialMarkets@macmillan.com.

First Edition: 2023

Printed in the United States of America

0 9 8 7 6 5 4 3 2 1

For Deepak

PART
ONE

CHAPTER ONE

When they tell him that everything looks to be in order—no abnormalities, no red flags, in great shape for his age—he feels, along with relief, a secret disappointment. He had hoped they would find something. And this hope afforded him a sense of importance, albeit unconsciously, that they would find something and then do what needed to be done. Recommend a diet. Exercise. Three pills a day. Measures he had been looking forward to but still would have resisted at first, before ultimately following eagerly. But now? What is he supposed to do? They present him with their findings, he takes them.

Now is the point where he could bring up how hard it is for him to get up in the morning, but they are already leading him out of the exam room, back into the waiting room, where he wishes he could stay. It's such a pleasant space. They clearly put a lot of time and effort into making it that way. On the walls are photos of babies in budding flowers, and oh, how he'd love to stay right here in front of them. Love to consider how on earth they managed to get inside, these babies with little butterfly wings. This is something else he could ask the doctor about, his tendency to sit and ponder question after question after question without any of it making sense, and whether that doesn't fit with some illness or other, and the fact that he can't get any peace from this barrage of questions, least of all in the morning, when this senselessness presses down on his chest the second he opens his eyes.

But maybe this is normal? Something to do with age? And maybe it will take some time—which, of course, he has plenty of now—to get used to? He takes his coat off the rack, dark gray, nearly black. In the shop where he bought it, they told him the color had a timeless elegance about it—at once both classic and modern—and, the cut, too, had a certain simplicity very much in vogue but at the same time traditional and—

But none of this mattered when it came down to it. He kept this thought to himself, just as he did the thought that this was likely the last jacket he would buy, the last shirt, the last pair of shoes. These things, he thought, were enough. He no longer needs anything more. And this filled him with a sense of contentment, knowing he had only modest requirements, but a wistfulness too, in having arrived at the point he had always believed was so far away, the day when he had no desire to own anything anymore. That time had come. Funny. He sees it now, but also sees that he should consider himself lucky. Healthy, that's all that matters; stop looking at the clock, stop sighing, pull up the corners of your mouth. It almost hurts, the smile he puts on to leave the doctor's office. Like a little facial spasm, which is how he imagines phantom pain would feel.

It was his wife who'd urged him to go and get examined from head to toe. She said he was better safe than sorry, though she never said that *to* him anymore, but mumbled it past him instead, into space: "It would be something for you to do, at least." He hadn't wanted to hear the little jab in her words at first. It was only later, half-asleep, that he found himself being lined up most inconsiderately in a row of other people who had nothing better to do than go once a month to the doctor to complain about their aches and pains with others just like them and thereby escape, at least temporarily, the loneliness at the heart of what they were describing.

He could see them now, cheerfully blabbing away about their ailments, which technically speaking weren't ailments at all, and they knew this but clung to their pinching and stinging and smarting wounds anyway. "Pathetic!" With this word and the way he ejected it from his body—so to speak—he attempted to separate himself from the rest of them, but the more he repeated it, the weaker it sounded—"Pathetic! Pathetic! Pathetic!"—so that by the end, the word seemed to implicate him as well. And what hurt wasn't knowing that he belonged with them but rather the isolation that belonging to them implied. His lying in bed listening carefully for a movement on the other side of the wall, and knowing precisely because of the slightest creak that his wife was still awake. Knowing nothing more about her than that. And that he was not in a position to call out to her. The only thing that felt familiar anymore, the only thing binding them together, was the distance between them.

And now? He makes it look like he has a destination in mind. He sets off with great big strides, as if there's someone waiting for him and it's of the utmost importance that he arrives in a timely manner. He's tried going for walks, simply that, walking for the sake of walking—can't do it. The problem is his hands; he doesn't know what to do with them. When he sticks them in his pockets, it makes him feel like a student playing hooky, and when he lets them dangle, well, then he feels like a runaway monkey who just wants to get back to his cage.

And what's the point anyway? Of walking? His wife says it's so that his joints don't rust over from disuse. She sends him out of the house every day so he can go around a few blocks. Though he knows her well enough to understand what she really means, which is to get out of her way. So that's why he's gotten used to it; it's not such a terrible way to pass the time after all. The only thing is he doesn't walk, he runs—that distinction is important to him. If only he had a dog! Then walk—absolutely! A white Pomeranian he could pull along behind him, one of those fantasies that makes him forget to breathe for a minute, that's how much it cheers him, imagining holding a leash pulled tight. But okay, he understands.

His wife made him understand: first of all, a dog costs money; second, you fall head over heels for the animal and get too attached. It's childish. Third: no more vacations. Fourth: the mess. And fifth: at some point, he's going to die. What then? To which he replied—because it was the smallest thing compared to money, love, and death, and because he at the very least wanted to be right about this smallest thing—that they never went on vacation anyway, which made her laugh, and him too, but then suddenly she stopped, and so did he, and they spent the rest of the day in uncomfortable silence. He never mentioned the white Pomeranian again, and he makes an effort to think of it as little as possible. But sometimes it does happen, like when he was eating, for example, and his wife seemed to be able to tell just by the way he requested a little bit more salt. It's nice, actually: they make a good team. He thinks of something. She notices. He notices that she notices. And even if neither of them says a word about it, it's the same as if they were yelling to each other across the table.

CHAPTER TWO

But in fact, there is no one waiting for him, and it doesn't matter if he comes home too late or not. After two or three blocks of running at a nice clip, sweat is streaming down his forehead, and it's embarrassing to him that this made him so exhausted, because he has no reason to be. He could sit down somewhere after all, he could lean back and watch the clouds go by, but even this—he's tried—he just can't do it. Every time he does, his gaze catches on the wires and the way they cut the sky in two. And watching the birds flying through that divided sky makes him sad. So. Better to avoid all that, stay on his feet, and wipe his brow with the handkerchief he keeps on hand for such purposes.

He, who has no reason to sweat anymore, is sweating, the way he never once did in all those years when he was still working, and he makes a mental note to look this up as soon as he gets home. He'll surely find it under "sweating" and "retirement." A hormone disorder that isn't easy to spot on the blood tests he is carrying with him, and he wonders whether he should maybe go back to the doctor's tomorrow? To get checked out again? Or maybe he would be better off going straight to a bigger hospital? And looking for a specialist? No, he should look it up himself first. There are some things you just have to work out for yourself, and others that sort themselves out on their own.

From the day he left the office, with his suitcase full of junk—photos and keepsakes he had decorated his desk with, including a woodpecker who, when someone lifts him up, taps against a tree trunk—it never once occurred to him to call any of his former coworkers. He can still see their faces clear as day, and he still remembers each of their extensions by heart too, but to pick up the receiver, call them up and say hello? They might think he was a ghost, and he is terrified of the pause that would follow after he gives his name.

"Um, *who*?"

The old, "It's me." Except that phrase would stay lodged in his throat.

Whatever became of Itō?

The former employee who, already retired, visited them in the office every first of the month, and if the first of the month fell on a Saturday or Sunday, then the second or third, to talk about his motorcycle? About roaring through the countryside? Into the setting sun? With the city behind him, the city where they were all flailing to their deaths, and for what reason, really? His hypothesis: because they assumed this is how it should be, which wasn't actually true. In reality—and how seductively this sounded coming out of his mouth—they were "free."

They believed him at first, and someone or other would start to dream: "When I retire, I'm going to do it just like Itō!" But after a while, doubts began to creep in, and they wondered why he never showed up on his motorcycle. Or why it was never in any of the photos he proudly passed around, instead they just saw a mountain or river, partially covered by his thumb? Here was where he'd camped. No tent, no firepit. There he'd almost gone into the ditch. A street without any curves, straight as an arrow. Each of Itō's retellings was more adventurous than the next, until finally they turned into a joke.

As soon as he left, a little hunched as he slipped out the door, they burst into laughter: "Him, on a motorcycle! At best, he takes the train, and even then you know he gets an upset stomach!" And it didn't matter to them whether he caught on or not, because they hardly missed him when he failed to show up by the fourth of the month. The sweet peaches he brought back for them from one of his "trips," as he took care to say, lay shriveled in a bowl on the table in the break room. One man joked: "He definitely bought these from the shop around the corner." And they shriveled up as the days went by, brown and juiceless, until at some point the cleaning lady threw them into the trash, her mouth twisted in disgust, where they landed among the lunch scraps, looking like shrunken heads.

He thinks of Itō a lot these days. Especially when he turns a corner and a gust of wind suddenly hits him in the face and ruffles his hair, like what happened just now, so that he can't breathe, only gasp and splutter and wheeze, and brace his upper body against his invisible opponent. Every time this happens, he resolves to look in on him, though not today—no, he's already been through enough—but soon, very soon, maybe tomorrow or the day after. It's on his list. At the top: *Call the kids. Ask how they're doing.* Then: *Fix the radio. Organize the records.* Though he's still on the fence about whether to sort them alphabetically or by genre. *Repot the bonsai.* But he's not so sure how. So then: *Look up how to do that.* A little farther down: *A present.* He had not added: *For my wife,* but instead: *For no particular reason,* because he heard, on the television program that he doesn't actually ever watch, that the best kind of gift-giving is when you surprise someone, as simple as that, without making yourself and your gift-giving the center of attention, which is unfortunately the case with most people, roughly 95 percent. Farther down: *Unpack the rolling suitcase* and, with a smiley face, *No more tripping over it! :) Look in on Itō. Spontaneously!!!* He added the three exclamation points later, you can tell by the different-colored ink. *De-moss the front steps. Get the roof checked. ~~Consider possible renovations, i.e. an addition.~~*

He crossed that out as soon as he wrote it. Just like the white Pomeranian. Except he never wrote that down in the first place, because what isn't written down can't be crossed out, which is a comfort to him, that he didn't have to cross it out, and more than that, a secret victory: "Ha, you think I'll give him up, but you are mistaken, ha! You are mistaken once again, my dear!" He catches himself saying things like this, but always quietly, and only ever to himself, and it always gives him a start, as if he is only just realizing who he's speaking to, and as if it's not him speaking, but someone else he doesn't know, someone who wants to stomp the whole house into the ground, including the steps and the roof, including the addition, the one that hasn't been built.

Quick, into the alley. Here he has a break from the wind. And why not walk somewhere different for a change? It's the detours, the many detours, that make this route interesting. That's something else he got from TV, a talk show "about life and how to master it." People should have the courage to abandon the beaten track for new ones so that they can feel like explorers. In the suburb he's lived in for over forty years, there are corners he's never noticed before, and it seems to him that he's realizing for the first time where his home is, after only going to the train station and back for decades, to the train station and back, hardly ever looking up, hardly ever looking closely at anything. Not a bad place. No, not at all. Just a suburb. A little boring, but it has everything you could ever need.

A new gym celebrated its grand opening a little bit ago, located conveniently close to the senior center, and there were brochures and pink balloons for people to take. When he went by, someone pressed one into his hand, and, not wanting to be rude, he walked around with it for a little while with a sheepish grin, as if he sought to apologize to anyone and everyone walking toward him for the way he must look: an elderly man holding a pink balloon. If someone were to have asked him—and he imagined for a moment the way they would have stopped him and then asked—he would have replied, without hesitation: "Oh, this? This is for my granddaughter!" And they would have taken him for a silly old grandfather, for he'd have immediately started singing the little girl's praises, going on about how smart she was, not yet three and already writing the hiragana Japanese script, it's just that no one asked him, and secondly, he doesn't have a granddaughter.

Young people these days! They're taking their time starting families. They don't seem to care too much about the whole thing, and if they do end up getting around to it, then either the sperm are too lazy or the eggs too . . . too—he can't think of a word for it—and the whole thing, which is fundamentally simple, becomes very complicated. At least that's what his wife insinuated, though in reality she surely knows more than that: that their children or their partners, most likely their partners, have "problems downstairs." And that's what he thought of when he let go of the balloon and let it rise into the air, watching it go until it burst with an inaudible pop. That his son and daughter, when he talked with them on the phone and asked how they were, always replied with a monosyllabic "good," and nothing more, making it impossible to draw the conversation out any further, which would have closed some of the distance between them. As soon as he hangs up, he can't remember anymore what they talked about, but this doesn't leave him with any regret, just relief: he's checked something off his list.

CHAPTER THREE

There's a taxi stand out front, and a taxi driver pops into his mind. The one who brought him home that night shortly before his retirement, after he managed to regain some of his senses. It cost a fortune, and he's ashamed to this day. He could tell from the man's accent that he came from Kansai, picked up on this right away, of course, even in his not yet fully sober state, and proceeded to explain that he came from there himself, he moved away as a child but still knew a few local expressions, this and that. The phrases felt familiar and reminded him of his mother.

"Oh yeah? They remind you of your mother?"

The driver's interest seemed sincere. And this emboldened him to tell him more about her, in a way he had never spoken about her to anyone before, including a little about how upset she could get sometimes: "It was unbelievable, how angry she got!" And that when it happened, she'd slip back into the dialect she'd tried so hard to abandon years ago, and that this would temper the effect of her anger a bit and made him feel warm instead, so that he'd yearn to be yelled at again long after he'd grown up, that's how good she was at the art of disciplining without doing real harm. Which was undoubtedly because of where she came from, the way she spoke, and undoubtedly because of her way of being in the world, which had been shaped by both.

It was at this point that he had begun to cry. Cautiously at first, more like a laugh, but then he began to sob. In the end, he was crying like a lost child. The taste of the tears. A little salty. Suddenly, it came rushing back to him, how it tasted when you cried. And the driver? He just kept driving. Turned on his right blinker, then the left. Passed back a tissue without saying a word, to where he sat cowering into himself in the back seat, said, "Shh," then fell silent again. Braked gently, then continued driving. The way he gripped the steering wheel, holding it with just the tips of his fingers, in this way staying precisely in his lane, not allowing himself to become guilty of anything. If only one could go through life this way! He thought that would be nice.

Once he regained his composure, they spoke of trivial things, the weather, the economy, and he was so sober now, so clear of fog, that he knew exactly which stock shares cost what. The new prime minister. What he thought of him? Honestly? That he was fighting to keep up with the Americans but falling behind, completely winded. They spoke the way you do about topics you know nothing about whatsoever, happy when the other nods, happy that all they did was show their approval without making a big thing of it, even when you know for a fact you haven't earned it. And then all at once, they were in front of the house.

They arrived, and he would love more than anything to just ask him to keep driving—before he gets out, the driver says he still has to show him something. Shows him pictures of his children that he pulls out of his wallet, one face after the next. He admires their features. He looks clever; she is such a cutie! This guy looks a little stubborn, but that's nothing to worry about, he'll grow out of it. And they laugh. Roar with laughter into the night.

His wife said later, "You woke up the whole neighborhood!" But why should it matter? If someone laughs? If someone laughs with their whole heart? "Let the whole world wake up!" Which she didn't find funny. But he did. And that's what he's clinging to now: that in this city there is a taxi driver who at this very moment is probably sitting in morning traffic and humming or whistling a tune—in short, that there is someone who knows something about him and will keep this bit of information close to his chest, humming and whistling as he does.

He is in the alley. Nothing surprising here. But he has it in his head that he's an explorer. If he had a voice recorder, he would narrate: "A cat jumps off the fence. Has a hunch there is fish somewhere in the bushes. A woman on a cane, I'll pass her soon. A cafeteria. Today, they're serving seafood curry." His explorer's spirit tires quickly, and he hurries to get back to the main road. The woman on the cane, seen now from the front, has a face that doesn't fit with the rest of her body, so colorfully made up in the hues of a bird of paradise, a purple streak of hair in the middle of sparkling white. When she smiles at him, he thinks she might fly away, that's the kind of lightness he sees in her smile, and wonders why he isn't able to do the same, what with the bill of health under his arm, the already slightly wrinkled findings.

Why is he entirely unable to smile? Or is it precisely for that reason? Because he has nothing to show for himself? Nothing that he can lay solemnly on the kitchen table that would authorize him to gather his wife and children around him and open it? And say that from now on—*now!*—everything has to change. Or else. Who knows? It might be too late. They would have to stick together in this moment of need, the future depends on it. And didn't they know already? That he needs them? No? "Well, you know *now*!" And one more time, with a tremor in his voice, so that they would remember this for a long time and think back on it as the moment everything changed, and then a little slower, for the record, so that they would be able to feel it like someone was writing on their skin: "I need you!" Then silence.

A deep, dark silence, which he would be the first to break. If someone were to beat him to it, he would forbid them to speak if it came to that. "It's my turn now." And so he would interrupt them, laying the medical findings neatly on top of each other and smoothing them out a few times as quietly as possible with his finger, his hand, or his forearm, whatever the case may be. A gesture with the deliberateness of an accountant, which would betray his emotion, and he can see it all now, see the way his wife is coming toward him, his children rushing in behind her. Then, end scene! He doesn't see anything else. His eyes are wet. A small part of him feels ashamed for how emotional this makes him.

CHAPTER FOUR

The homeless man is at the intersection. He is the only one they have here, a sort of living monument, not very nice to look at, but people have grown used to him and tolerate him, because he's the only one and because he doesn't—as they initially feared—disturb the local charm of the place. Instead, he imparts a certain romantic quality, what with his tangled hair a bird could make a nest in and the black creases of his neck. What's more, over time he has essentially made himself useful. People give him old and unwanted things, and he accepts them with gratitude, which then allows the person to say about themselves in good conscience: *I gave something away.* Take his old suit, for instance, with the worn-out spots on the arms. The man's been wearing it these past few months, and while it's strange to see him in it, the suit met a worthy end. To throw it away, no—it was still in too good of shape for that, an Italian make anyway, Salvatore or something, and he thought long and hard over whether it would be worth patching. But to give it away, that was a deed that made the world a little bit better.

He always says hello to him, and that also makes it better: "Hello, how are you?"—"Good. And you? Divorced yet?" His usual joke. And he doesn't hold it against the homeless man but assumes his role eagerly as if he owes it to him. "Tsk-tsk-tsk"; the homeless man looks at him sympathetically: "Retirement doesn't suit you. Your wife has to be getting fed up. Send word when it happens. I'll represent you!"—"I'll do that."—"Please do!"

It's always the same lines, thrown out quickly in passing, and he knows he shouldn't take it seriously, but in spite of himself, there are some days he's consumed by superstition: the homeless man, who is still in his suit, might actually be his proxy, and his wife might actually be happier bunking with him, the proxy, down by the river, than in her own home up in the village. The homeless man seems to sense this. Sometimes he calls out, "No harm meant!" once he has already gone by. Sometimes not.

On days like today, he walks for a while a ways behind him, apologizes multiple times, bowing like a servant, and he can smell him, that's how close he is, a mixture of river grass, damp soil, and something else he can't place, the man's strong instincts maybe, and for a split second, not longer, he envies him the freedom of his existence, the privilege to be a fool, under the great big sky, to nourish himself off what passersby extend to him, to sit on top of a cardboard box and not be in anyone's way. He doesn't have anyone who sends him out of the house. Nor, for that matter, does he have a house at all.

Where is my handkerchief?

He just had it . . . He turns out his jacket pockets. It's not there. His pants' pockets are—now, can that be?—still sewed shut. He begged his wife over and over again to pull out the threads, but she keeps putting it off. And she certainly has enough time! What else does she do all day? Apart from going grocery shopping, not a whole lot, but what does he know? Nothing, it seems. "This is the last straw!" When he gets home, he'll make her answer for this. That's the first thing he'll do. Plant himself in front of her—there—his shoulders squared a bit, arms lifted slightly from his sides—and ask her what this means—does she intend for him to walk around with sewed pockets for the rest of his days, or even better, *live* with sewed pockets for the rest of eternity? And he doesn't want to have to ask again. The fact that he has to even ask in the first place. Infuriating. Sweat is running down his neck and back, now even his medical results are wet from his sweaty armpits. He needs to sit down somewhere. Right now. Catch his breath.

Suddenly, he is very tired. But there is no bench in sight. *Typical suburb,* he thinks. You're outside in nature and aren't allowed to sit or look—or do anything at all, for that matter. There isn't even anywhere to sit outside the train station, probably so no one gets the idea to linger longer than they should. There used to be a plastic bench with the faded logo of a beverage company that has since gone bankrupt, and he remembers a group of teenagers for whom this was not a bench but a couch.

When he came home from work, he was always happy to see them hanging around there, being bored together, barely even glancing at him—he could have been their father after all, and it wouldn't have made a difference to them. In spite of this, their apathy struck him as friendly, which was why he missed them when one night they disappeared along with the bench, and he still wonders where they are, whether they are still together or scattered to the wind—he likes to believe, against his better judgment, that they stayed together. Back when it happened, he'd written a letter to the city. The bench should be returned. The teenagers need a spot where they can sit and stare into space. No one ever responded to the letter, but he still has the carbon copy. Whenever he comes across it when he's cleaning, it surprises him every time. That at one point in time he bothered to write something like that.

So. Back home, sans handkerchief, get to the bottom of the pocket issue. But he takes a different route because he doesn't want to see the homeless man again, at least not when he's this sweaty. Nor does he care to go through the alley where the woman with the cane smiled at him, or the corner where he had to think about Itō. And so he walks along the cemetery, the one next to the railroad tracks, and because he still has more than an hour until lunch, he resolves to give "going for a stroll" another try. Practice does make perfect when all's said and done.

So. He ducks through the cemetery gate, slows his pace. Anyway, he is in the presence of the dead here, and this thought helps him to concentrate on his breathing. Just get to that grave there. He has purpose. He wants to go slowly—very slowly—until he reaches it. Relaxes his jaw. That's good. Twists his neck until it cracks. His hands? Doesn't matter where they go! There's no one here to make him feel self-conscious. Let them dangle. The dead enjoy this. "That's right! You guessed it, I'm an ape!" And he imagines the dead poking each other in the side, their rickety laughter spurring him on. "You want more? Here, how's this?" He drums his fists against his chest, just trying it out at first, then in earnest, says, "Ooh-ooh!" and "Aah-aah!" and

"Ooh-ooh!" whereby his medical findings float to the ground and he, transformed into a wild animal, tramples all over them until they're covered in dust.

A train rattles by. For a moment, he worries someone might recognize him, but his mouth is already wide open: "You, train driver!" He screams this. "At some point, you'll all end up here!" And he stomps—no, he's dancing now, he fell into a dance step without realizing it. He trips nimbly along in narrower and narrower circles, not an ape anymore, no, but a dying swan. Like the one in the ballet his wife dragged him to before they were married so that he could learn—as she put it—"*who I am.*" And he had sat there in the darkness, in that cough-filled room, and had not been able to understand what she'd meant.

He found it perfectly lovely. The ballerina could have been a little more attractive. That big mole on her leg, he couldn't stop staring—could she not have had it removed? Or concealed at least? But for the sake of his wife, in profile, an image he still remembers, and that single tear on her cheek when the curtain fell, he had done his best to show that he was moved as well. His first lie. The very first. And she believed him. Was moved by his being moved and when he brought her home granted him a somewhat-passionate kiss and somewhat-passionate hug, whereby for him the only reason the performance stayed in his mind at all was because that night was the first time he felt under her shirt, the first time she let him do as he liked. "Really? You really feel that way about me?" To which he exclaimed, "Of course I do!" and pressed her up against the door.

Everything unfolded from there. They married not long after. When people asked them what they liked about each other, a question people enjoy posing to young couples, he responded: "How deeply she thinks about everything." And she: "That he interrupts me when I'm thinking deeply about something." And they enjoyed the bafflement that followed, which made them feel special and unique, until people stopped asking, stopped asking very quickly, and so their responses lost their novelty just as quickly, if not sooner.

CHAPTER FIVE

Scampering around one last time, he throws his arms into the air. His fingertips graze the clouds, which just a moment ago had pushed in front of the sun, which shone so brightly when it broke through them again that his chest felt like it had caught on fire. Burning, he sinks to one knee, his other leg stuck out in front of him, lets his arms fall slowly, one last beat of his wings, then he is scorched. *Now just don't fall over,* he thinks, teetering slightly. Hold this tension. Hold it. Hold it as long as possible. Something occurs to him: there's a lot of space between each grave, enough space that you can stay out of each other's way. He teeters again. Someone is clapping.

He rises, blinded by the sun, brushes the dust off his knees. Who could that be? He squints. A woman. But not his wife? In his confusion, this seems possible. He expects to find a trace of similarity, even from as far away as he is, in the way she steps out of the tree's shadow, like she's extricating herself from it, stepping into the blazing light, as if by doing so she means to say: "I caught you!"

"I'm sorry," he wants to shout, but all he can do is clear his throat.

The young woman—she is still clapping—is standing in front of him now, laughing—still laughing.

"That was great," she says. "You just need a little more oomph! But aside from that, you're good enough to join a circus."

"Thank you!" He says this in spite of himself. Now he must somehow be rid of her, must for his own sake bring the whole thing quickly to an end, as gracefully as possible. He bows. "The dance is finished."

"No, it can't be!" She wanted to see more.

"More next time."

"You do this a lot, do you?"

Because of the way she says this, suddenly serious, and the way she looks him up and down with her tongue between her lips as if it's helping her make sense of him, he feels strangely uplifted. She's looking at him with a little bit of a smirk, sure, but there is a hint of recognition as well, and he tries his best to meet her gaze just as directly, to look her dead in the eyes, which is actually very difficult, because in her heels she towers over him, and moreover, she is wearing a tight shirt with I'M UP HERE! written across it, along with an upward arrow.

"Are you still with me? Hello?" She waves both hands in front of him as if they weren't standing inches from each other but instead a great distance apart, on the opposite end of the cemetery.

He rushes to pull himself together, to mumble something or other, something that might distract her, compel her to leave him alone. Does he do this a lot? she asks again. He answers dryly, "No," but then, because he can see she is disappointed, he turns the question back on her: "And what about you? Do you do this a lot? Hide behind a tree and spy on strangers?"

"Actually, yes, you could say that's part of my job."

"Aha."

He suspected as much. But now he's trapped without a clear escape route. *No follow-up questions,* he thinks. *Drop it. Don't show any interest. I'm not buying whatever she's selling.* But the young woman—midtwenties, most likely, and judging by how self-assured she is maybe even a little older—seems to be having fun backing him into a corner.

"Don't worry," she says with a wink, something he last saw in a sixties Hollywood movie. "It's nothing inappropriate. I'm an actor, I guess you could say, and observing people is a kind of hobby that I've turned into a job. You learn a lot that way. About yourself as well. In fact, it's mainly that. When I saw you dancing, for instance, I realized that I don't spend enough time in my own body. Do you know what I mean by that?"

He cocked his head.

"That! Exactly that—you were acting like you were trying to understand, so you tilted your head to the side, when in fact you aren't in your head at all. You are actually thinking, *No,* which means your gesture is just an empty one. Do you follow?"

"Yes."

He nods to avoid making the same mistake again.

"Still, the person inside here, look, here"—she taps her finger on the tip of her nose—"is pretty impressive, and I mean that sincerely. That's important in my profession. Otherwise, you blow your cover." After a pause, she adds, "I suppose that applies to life as well."

Is that right? Does he see it that way too? He focuses on being in his body. Stands up straighter so he doesn't feel so small in front of her. "This is all very interesting, but . . ."

"I know, you have to go. Just one last thing." And as she says this, she moves toward him, first one step, then another, and another, and as she gets closer, she begins to whisper: "The truth is, though, that you actually *don't* need to go. And deep down, here"—she puts her hand on his chest—"you're curious about what it is that I do, you just don't believe that you truly want to know. Though," she runs the back of her hand along his arm, "it would be something for you as well! Yes, I really think you would be p-e-r-f-e-c-t for it." And with that, she withdraws her hand and takes a step back, laughing, asks him, as he stands there, dumbstruck: "Now, how was that? Not so bad after all, hm? My favorite role. A crazy woman. Sadly, she isn't requested all that often."

The way she is looking at him, cautiously inquisitive, reminds him of his wife when she is intent on explaining something he already understands, but will not reveal he understands. The patience it takes for him to do that: give it up. His defiance. Waiting so long for someone you know will come walking around the corner eventually.

"Well then. I want to know. Do tell: What exactly do you do?"

This seems to surprise the young woman. She bites her bottom lip. Then, suddenly unmasked and visibly relieved, she takes a deep breath and says: "I play family."

A sentence he knows for a fact will stay with him, he knows this as soon as it comes out of her mouth—this is the kind of sentence that keeps him up at night, keeps him tossing and turning to the point where all he wants is to say to his wife through the wall, "Just come over here. Enough with all this. We can put it all behind us; holding on to all our little problems isn't doing us any good." A sentence as straightforward as it is to declare: He's never gotten used to sleeping in separate bedrooms. He finds himself longing for her to steal the blankets like she used to; nowadays, he can't believe that was something they used to fight about. There are more important things after all, for instance—well, the pockets occur to him.

"Family?" he hears himself say. "But you can't 'play' something like that."

"Oh, but you can. If only you knew. The requests are non-stop. Last night, for instance, it was one of those guys who you could tell, just from talking on the phone, that he wears ties with funny patterns. Anyway, he's getting married and needs a sister who can talk about his childhood at the wedding. About how great of an older brother he is, always there to get me out of a jam. One time, imagine this, he saved me from coating myself in superglue. I was five at the time and thought it was lipstick. And if he hadn't been there, I wouldn't be able to give a speech about him today. You see? I'm his little sister. A little sappy, but sweet, especially because I get a little bit of a lisp when I'm nervous. That's a little quirk he requested. The guests should enjoy themselves after all."

"And his parents? I mean, they can't be expected to go along with this."

"Both dead. Some kind of accident."

"And his wife?"

"She already knows all about it. She likes the idea. A sister-in-law she can show off, though of course she can't be better-looking than she is. But anyway, to avoid potential confusion,

I live abroad, somewhere in Hawaii I think, it was Kalahi or Kaluhu or someplace like that, I still have to double-check on that in case someone asks. We're meeting up tomorrow, my brother and I, to go over final details. Things like names, places, relationships with relatives. And my, or the sister's, name is Mie."

"That's a nice name."

"Yeah, don't you think? I personally would have preferred something a little more flowery, but oh well, that's the way it works, the customer asks and they shall receive. So, I am Mie—it's a pleasure to meet you." She gives a little curtsy. "I've been four other people before this. And after, whew! There's a long list. I am a niece, a cousin, and an aunt, and sometimes all over the course of just three days. Very rarely a wife, though occasionally the new one. Most often a girlfriend. I was a granddaughter for the first time today! Yep, that's right: before I came here, I was with a woman who booked me as her granddaughter. She said all she wanted was to look at the smooth skin of a young person again, and so we sat across from each other drinking tea, without saying much. It was nice, actually, but afterward, I'm not sure why, I was in the mood for the cemetery."

They laughed. He louder than she.

"Your outfit isn't exactly grandma-appropriate."

"I mean, she wanted young, and this is young, and she liked it, the heels best of all! You might think it's funny, but she even tried them on, and the way she had to hold on to her cane made it all very touching."

"Her cane, you said?" He thought back to the bird of paradise from earlier.

"Yes." She blinked and quickly wiped her face. "She could

barely lift her feet. But none of that mattered; she was set on wearing high heels at least once in her life. For the sake of the view, she said. From up there—her words—she could see Mount Fuji."

"And? Will you see her again?"

He felt terrible imagining the old woman sitting alone in her apartment with two mugs in front of her, half-empty and half-full, the leftover smile on her face drooping slowly, very slowly, without her noticing. Wouldn't she be lonelier now than before? A little older, perhaps?

"No." Mie's voice had returned to the way it must sound when she is explaining her operation to a customer, recommending one package over another. "The instructions are clear: no attachments. And this is what it means: Imagine I'm playing a person from their innermost circle, but a few years down the road, let's say, because right now this wouldn't be taken seriously—I'm the mother of a daughter who wants to put some fire under her boyfriend's butt. I, the mother, happen to run into him on the street, and the whole time we're talking I am embodying a particular emotion—in this case, concern—as to whether he's truly the right man for my daughter, about where he comes from, his family background, what he studied, how he's dressed, whether he treats my daughter the way I feel she deserves to be treated—though the relationship itself stays between the two of them.

"A tightrope act, if you like. I insert myself yet remain on the periphery. Any conceivable consequences—like whether he does or does not in fact get a move on, or whether when he meets the real mother later, he asks why she's acting like she's never seen him before—anything like that is for the girl to deal with, she has to work it out herself. I'm simply filling a hole, nothing more.

"Anything more and I'd be derelict in my duties, because it would upset the balance of the relationship. Or did that not occur to you? That upon meeting a person for the second time, someone would assume they already knew them? This is precisely what's dangerous about it: someone starting to feel a sense of familiarity."

She still sounds businesslike.

"Pretty callous," he says, and he wishes she would go back to talking in a softer tone. It suits her better than when she's just reciting facts.

"Callous? Well, yes. I don't know. Still, I have to protect myself, but not just myself, my team too. We can be confidential, but not familiar. We lend a hand, but a gloved hand. My team? You really want to know? Right now, we're eight women, myself included, and three men, except that one of them, a film student, will switch to his actual subject soon. We're still small, but we're growing, and my dream is that in a few years we'll be the best. Interested? Here's our card."

She opens a purse embroidered with sparkly rhinestones that he hadn't noticed before; funny, it was tucked in the crook of her arm the whole time, maybe because she is sparkling herself, he thinks, and takes the card almost gingerly as if it were a toad that might not be poisonous but is still horrifying nonetheless, with all its warts and its meaty neck and suction cups. Red lettering in the shape of a feather runs along the edge of the card onto the back, where it ends in the middle in a bow:

"Happy Family," he reads, a relief printing. He runs his finger over it, pausing at each letter.

"Our slogan," she chimes in eagerly as if she wants to interrupt him, even though he hasn't begun to say anything. "We help people feel a sense of belonging. The foundation of happiness!"

No name, no address, just a phone number. What is he supposed to do with this?

"Call and make an appointment," she jokes. "Maybe at some point, you'll need a daughter to wish her father a happy Father's Day? Or a colleague with whom you can vent about your boss over a beer, or maybe a few?" Oh, he isn't working anymore? "Even better! Then apply for a job with us! I mean that in all seriousness. Some extra income once in a while, something you can put away for later, like a trip, for instance. Pensions aren't anything special nowadays, you know. Or maybe for the feeling of being needed." Here she faltered for a moment, before continuing more quietly, "You strike me as someone who isn't needed for too much, or often enough, either."

"Bang!" He claps his hand to his chest and imitates the staggering of a cowboy dealt a deadly blow. "Now that hurt." He laughs, surprised at himself; his little performance escaped him before he could say anything. "But don't worry! I can take it." He wants to stick the card in his pocket, but rats, it's sewed shut! Who makes a cowboy joke with sewed-up pockets? He is instantly small again, feels himself growing smaller and smaller, just a dusty trace underfoot that he'll leave here amid the graves, between which wildflowers are growing, as flowers in vases people selected for this purpose wilt in putrid water. He promises to think about it. Though she should take back what she said about the circus.

"What, why?" Mie is adamant. "That was a compliment."

CHAPTER SIX

It is already afternoon by the time they say goodbye. High time to head back home. And on the way, he can't help but get a little agitated: you can't make these things up! The world is filled with such insanity. A young woman who has convinced herself she is selling the foundation of happiness, and not only that, she sparkles! She sparkles so much he almost bought it. Wait until he tells his wife! But she won't want to believe it, and the card won't be enough to prove it, least of all that he was doing ballet in a cemetery on a Monday afternoon, which he can't share with her under any circumstances, because she would ship him off to a psychiatrist.

Better to not say anything at all. Eat and keep his mouth shut. He remembers the couple he once sat next to in a restaurant, a bald man and a woman who couldn't stop playing with her hair. And because he was alone and bored, he had counted how many words they exchanged between them. It was three. *Tastes good* and *Mm-hmm,* though he only counted the third as half a word. A scene made even more comical, albeit unintentionally, by the fact that one table over was a group of deaf people who seemed to almost literally be hurling words at one another. Despite the silence enveloping them, they were clearly in the midst of a heated discussion. Mouths hanging wide open, though without a single sound escaping, hands slicing through the air, landing briefly on a forehead, cheek, or neck—just watching all this made him dizzy. If he'd had to pick one of the tables to join, a choice he posed to himself out of boredom, he wouldn't have moved, would have stayed exactly where he was, all by himself. No question. He still remembers his reasoning: *This is the safest option.*

The waitress brought out a tray with hot udon and tempura. When she set the bowl of noodles in front of him, he noticed that she did so without any special charm or care, purely mechanical, like a robot imitating the way a person moves. And as she did this, a little bit of soup spilled over the brim, not much, but enough to make him bark at her.

"Hey, careful!"

She shot him a glance, infinitely sad, a robot who understands it will never be human. And in the end, he was the one to apologize to her instead of the other way around, and he defended her to the manager, who had run over in the meantime. But her expression didn't change. It remained sad and cold, as if the sadness had coated every other feeling in a thick layer of ice.

The couple at the table next to him carried on their meal in silence. The deaf people were gesticulating like mad. He was on the verge of calling over to them: "Not so loud, please!" The manager gave him an extra helping of rice and shooed the waitress behind the bar, where she turned her back to him and busied herself with plates and glasses. The soft clinking filled him with something he hadn't felt in a long time. But what was it?

This kneading and tugging? He couldn't name it until a while later.

Homesickness.

Just one more hill! He has it in him. He just needs to lean forward a bit and push his feet harder off the ground, lifting off with each step, puffing as he goes. He honed his technique over the years, and some days, he can make it up without wheezing, and in no time at all. Today isn't one of those days. He has to stop at the deserted patch of land, crouch down, and let out a long exhale. Meanwhile, his gaze catches on the same thing it always does when he passes by, the rusty bicycle without tires or a seat—just a skeleton of a bike—standing there in the middle of the grass in the deserted patch—yes, standing!

It's still standing, he thinks every time he sees it, and wonders how it can be that it hasn't been blown over yet by a gust of wind—or a storm, for that matter; it seems to be defying gravity. And why hasn't anyone come to pick it up? There's the trash collection that disposes of bulky waste once a month—not even that? Maybe because this isn't a designated dumping spot? It's as if this particular patch of land weren't part of the neighborhood, just a narrow rectangle—an eyesore, as it's called at every neighborhood association meeting—that doesn't belong to anyone but instead to the mice.

And he always greets them, the mice, either as he's walking by or stopping for a quick rest, as he is now, a habit that over time has become a downright compulsion. He has to greet them, or else something will happen. Has to signal his greeting with some sort of gesture, like tipping his hat, though he isn't wearing one. He has to, because otherwise no one else will, and it is actually important to show mice respect in this way. Or else. He doesn't know what might happen. Maybe the bicycle would tip over at the slightest breeze. That's just how it is, and it affects him just the same as it does, he believes, everyone who lives there.

At the neighborhood meetings, he holds back when the topic comes up; only once did he chime in, weakly, that it would actually be nice if the eyesore stayed; they could avoid the hassle of moving it elsewhere, like in a neighbor's yard, for instance, at which point everyone stared at him uncomprehendingly, like someone who isn't quite right in the head. Since then, they've made it clear they take him for a lunatic, he can see it in their tolerant smiles when he walks up to his door in the evening, and by the women who happen to be standing there with their children, chatting, who suddenly pause, then pick up their conversation but at a different point, with the kind of smile that shows they're tolerating, but also mildly ignoring him.

He used to enjoy living so high above the village. They had been among the first people to sign up for the Living in the Sky project, compelled to do so because of how uniquely in love they considered themselves to be. They turned even the obvious downsides, like the long walk to the train station, and school, and the nearest grocery store, into positives: having to walk the hill would keep them spry in their old age, and who said they would live here forever? When they'd had enough, well, then they would just move to Paris! It was easy for them to say those kinds of things, and they reveled in the wide-eyed looks they got from people when they told them their plans. But the garret in Montmartre slowly turned into an apartment in Karuizawa, which would still be just as hip, and then Karuizawa turned into an indeterminate place in the south, until finally it wasn't a place at all, because they stayed where they were and lost the ability to imagine being anywhere else.

At least that is the case for him.

He is attached to this house that he might not have built himself but is nonetheless always tinkering around with in his head, and if and when his wife brings up a move, suggesting it is time, perhaps, to move back down to the town center, maybe even shows him a list of potential properties that an agent had put together for her—for she had gone to see an agent without consulting with him—then he feels attacked, as if someone is threatening to peel the skin off his body. When she lists her reasons—heavy grocery bags, something is always breaking, or the fact that nearly everyone else their age has already "downsized," as they say, to make room for the younger ones—he retorts, "Not me!" and it is the only *no* he utters, which leaves her with her hands tied, and makes him worry, secretly, that she could one day respond with, "Well then, I'll go without you!" Which makes him cling to it even more fiercely.

About this much he's certain: in an apartment, no matter here or in Paris, he would begin to die. It would start the process of his gradual wasting away. The precursor to an urn. Maybe that's what she means by "downsizing"? He, on the other hand, feels like "expanding." Their little patch of lawn. They could turn it into a rock garden, or, fine: a lawn is less maintenance. A little doghouse to go with it? That would be something! He already knows exactly the materials he would need, he can feel the wood in his hands, feels it yield as he saws through it. He smells the varnish. The blue stain. Sees the nameplate and the level he uses to adjust it, to millimeter precision. The white Pomeranian, meanwhile, is jumping up on him, and he makes sure he doesn't step on any loose nails lying around. Shiro, that's his name, obeys his every command. When he scolds him, "Calm down, Shiro!" Shiro pricks up his ears and tilts his head a little to the side, a sight that melts him every time. He is a clever dog. He knows how to pose to get his owner to scratch him behind the ears. And even when he doesn't say it out loud, this is the last thing he has to say on the matter: if *he* can't have a Pomeranian, then *she* can't have an apartment. That the one should preclude the other, he dismisses as a side matter.

The main thing: they are staying put.

CHAPTER SEVEN

The house. He approaches it the way you would a sleeping person. Cautiously. So as not to wake it. To watch it dreaming. It is the highest house in the village, its gable towers above the other houses', and it was worth the extra money—an understatement meant to make his wife understand that he had taken the decades-long loan to the bank happily in stride, and all he asks for in exchange is a little gratitude.

He had worked his whole life for this house—this is an exaggeration—and now that he is retired, he has finally reached the point where he can enjoy being home; this man should hawk it off me, off you, for a song? Insanity! She has to understand it would have all been for naught: Waking up every day, showering, boarding a train packed with commuters. Getting tossed here and there. Unable to find anything secure to hold on to. Feeling exhausted before you even get home. Agonizing, so tired, over stacks of papers pushed under his nose by the boss, a title that will never be his. Driving home at night with the sense he's only grasped half of it. Eating, another shower, then tiptoeing into the children's room for a glimpse at their faces. To see how much they've grown. Each one a spitting image of himself. The girl most of all; the boy bears a stronger resemblance to his mother, which doesn't bother him, though

he does acknowledge it would have been better if the opposite
were true.

Where would their lives take them? Further than his had
taken him? But maybe that wasn't even to be desired. At the
very least, he wishes them a normal life, by which he means a
contented life, without too much excitement, a life not unlike
his own, in a house like this one, with children just like them.
Sure, they could have it a little easier. But when it comes down
to it, it's not so terrible to have to suffer a little bit. Makes you
stronger. You can appreciate what you have only after you've
worked for it. Take weekends, for instance. You wouldn't know
how valuable they were if you didn't spend a whole week slav-
ing toward them, those two days spent comatose, dreaming the
children's noisy voices out of the house, where the children dis-
appear along with them, dreaming of the door shutting behind
them, and finally, silence, where he drifts, suspended, entirely at
peace with himself and everything around him, all the furniture
they've collected over the years, the textures he delights in: the
smooth sofa covering, smooth tabletop, smooth knickknacks on
the smooth bookshelves. All this smoothness! She has to understand that this is all just as it should be. A bill paid off without
anything left over. He climbs up the steps—the moss can stay; it
gives them a certain patina. WELCOME HAPPINESS! is written
on the doormat. He kicks off his shoes and some fine gravel. He
brought it back home with him from the cemetery.

His wife isn't home. He notices this at once. Her purse isn't on
the bureau, annoying that she always puts it there anyway, as if

it were too much for her to hang it up on the hook right next to it. Instead, a note. *Back soon,* he reads. *Food in the fridge. Needs to be warmed up.* It takes a second for these simple words to register, and he rereads them aloud to get to the bottom of them. *Back soon*—but back from where? *Food in the fridge*—but not something already made? *Needs to be warmed up*—but how? On the stove?

He begins by first not getting worked up, because what's the point, who is he supposed to be angry with? There's no one here. His face is reflected at him in the smooth mirror, red from his walk. That wrinkle is new, he thinks, and brings his forehead closer to the glass, so close it's almost touching. The gray at his temples, on the other hand, that's been there for some time, since he was about forty, and he often considered dyeing it, until it got to a point where it would have looked ridiculous; he should have done it from the start. Not like that bald man he spent every morning with on the train, then one day barely recognized because of a shiny black toupee, and who has since remained a stranger, so much so that he stopped nodding to him over his newspaper as he had always done before, he simply couldn't manage it—a friendly nod for this former acquaintance.

Better this way. Let nature run its course. Accept the aging process, because there's just no way around it. And besides, he has to smile, remembering what people used to say to him, women, giggling that the gray gave him a kind of daring: "You men! You have it good. You just get better with age. We women, on the other hand! Oh, it's not fair." At which point, he pinched the woman's cheek until she cried out, laughing, as if he had hurt her. The slap he got in return, oh, he'd earned that, and later, he turned it into a story that he recited as often and as loudly as he could, although he switched out a few details after the fact, like the cheek for a butt, the slap for an unexpected punch to the chest, which resulted in peals of laughter—the hostess who turned out to be a boxer. Who would have suspected. The others who had been there even helped him work out further details, adding some, omitting others, wishing they had seen something different. And by the end, it had become something of a legend, with each person responsible for their respective part, the hostess herself even chiming in for dramatic effect, something along the lines of her getting the distinct sensation she was sending her fist through his chest into empty space, shocked to find there was nothing there, no muscles, no flesh, just a hole where his heart should have been. But no one found this funny, so they deleted it again. Replaced his chest with his soft tissue. Laughed about it for months. A running gag that at some point ran its course. In the end, all he managed to inspire were yawns.

CHAPTER EIGHT

His slippers. He feels at home the second he slides into them. The insoles have molded to the shape of his feet, and although the brown leather toe cap is completely tattered and the brown only brown in retrospect, it is the insoles that keep him from parting with the shoes. He inherited them from his father, and if it were up to his wife, they would have gone in the trash along with everything else, the newspapers and heaters and pots and pans, but he kept them because they were the first thing that caught his eye upon entering his parents' house—how lonely they looked there in the hallway, one of the few personal items his father left him, aside from the cheap watches and a small notebook where his father noted the time and consistency of each of his bowel movements, whether there was blood or not. He'd had a hard time putting on the slippers at first because his father's toes, every last one, had burrowed deep into the footbed, so deep that when he wore them, he seemed to fall into his same shuffling gait, and his wife complained they made him look like an old man. But after a while, his own impression began to superimpose his father's, and he could feel the exact and irreversible point when the slippers switched over to their new owner, and after that, they belonged irrevocably to him, the son. He *loves* them. He knows how foolish this sounds. But he does, he loves them for their malleability and because they help him, in moments like these—when he's finally made it home, famished and sweaty—to think briefly of his father and of how nice it would be to see him again if they happened to meet today.

There wouldn't be any trace of the hate from back in the day, from when he learned, by accident and far too late, that his mother was still alive. An uncle let it slip. A moment of negligence that didn't erase those years of lies but still left him with the distinct feeling that his mother had actually been quite close by the entire time. This woman who had never gotten truly upset with him, because that would require some level of affection to have been there in the first place. Just the fact that with the cabdriver he wanted to stick to the version where he'd wished as a boy for a mother who was strict because of her love for him, who would have given him a spanking if it was deserved. The truth made her sound so sleazy in comparison. Instead of getting mad or spanking him, she took one man after another into her bed, then finally ran off with one of them, and when she disappeared, his father had simply declared her dead, because he considered this better. A fact, period, that didn't leave any room for contradiction. It takes a lot to not hate the liar after that.

For all those years of believing her dead, when instead he could have been holding on to hope that she might return, that one day he would open his eyes to find her sitting there at the kitchen table with her usual indifference—how he missed that!—barely lifting her gaze to wish him a good morning. How much easier it would have been for him to get through those dark nights. He still gets choked up whenever he thinks about it, but then he just slides into his slippers and finds he can pass over this memory with relative calm, which is the reason he doesn't like wearing the slippers his wife buys him every year for his birthday, which gets her complaining all over again that he is a stubborn old man. This year, he pushed *Give me something else* into her room on thin washi paper, through the crack in the door, and it should have been a joke and should have compelled her to come out laughing, even if reproachfully, but what came out of her room instead was a pile of shreds, a shame about the paper, he'd thought, pressing his ear to the door. Could she actually be crying? He hadn't been able to tell whether the sniffing he heard was from tears or anger. In his pajamas, he felt suddenly like a stranger in his own home, and he strained to hear some other sound that would have allowed him to knock until there was nothing more to hear, and so he backed slowly away from the door—maybe she would still come out?—and returned to his room next door. "It was just a joke!" he repeated quietly to himself as he set the slippers next to his bed. And he seemed to mean it. Not a hint of laughter.

He opens the fridge. Everything is there. Even labeled. So that he, the idiot, doesn't have to go hungry. He reads: *Microwave, two minutes!* And on the microwave: *Turn to medium!* Chopsticks and salt—likely for the event that he desires a pinch more—are already set out on the table. Beside them the paper for afterward, opened already to the right spot, the weather report, which he always studies first, not after breakfast but after lunch, because he likes to be surprised in the event of an afternoon shower. A habit left over from the old days when they felt bold enough to just brave it, umbrella-less, even if there were clouds hanging heavy in the sky, and then when the downpour started, they didn't bother taking cover because they wanted to get soaked instead.

Or at least that's how it had happened once when he had joined in too: they were standing at an intersection with people fleeing all around them, and they had thrown up their hands high in the sky, intertwined, just like in the movie where the man and woman—French people who smoked a lot, cigarettes and love their only sustenance—were killed in an accident just a few seconds later. It was the closing scene, he still remembers the music exactly, a mournful waltz, just as he remembers the way the camera captured their bodies, how they started to stagger through the rain in sheer happiness, tottering blissfully in a way that seemed it would never end, until the screen went black and you heard the muffled sound of a collision.

"What nonsense is this!" He was irate. "Are they so stupid they just go stumbling into a car? And after three hours where nothing happens, absolutely nothing!"

But that's life. His wife explained it to him: nothing happens, nothing happens for a long time, and then, all of a sudden, everything comes to a stop. That was back when she was expecting their first child. This was their last chance to go crazy! Before it was too late! It was her idea to act out the scene. She walked with him down the hill to the train station, her belly already round as a ball; it was the only intersection in the suburb suitable for a backdrop, and she insisted they stand close—"Very close," she said—to the curb. And he was anxious, not because

of the two, three cars barreling toward them at twenty kilome-
ters an hour but because of the enthusiasm he saw in her eyes,
which had a certain craziness about it, when she turned back
to him with her hair dripping wet and asked over her shoulder
what was the matter with him, couldn't he stand this little bit of
rain for her, what was his problem, did he think she was crazy?
Before he pulled her tenderly to him and folded her even more
tenderly in his arms, and she cried and cried, seemingly without
end, water flowing down over them both.

CHAPTER NINE

"Tastes good," he murmurs. But it would have been better fresh. Especially the eggplant, which had become a little too mushy after being heated up. He didn't like when food fell apart before he could get it into his mouth, least of all vegetables, which tended to fall apart regardless. If she had just served them on a separate plate! Then he wouldn't have had to put them in the microwave with everything else. But that hadn't occurred to her—*Back soon!*—which is why the issue of the pockets took on even more weight.

It's obvious she's been a little off lately—he's noticed this after paying closer attention—she's letting certain things slip, which, if it goes on for too long, won't be able to be put right again. A sloppiness she must have picked up from someone else, because this certainly was not the person he married, and no matter how much times might have changed, some things simply can't be permitted. Like her opening the newspaper to the correct spot, for instance, but then forgetting to lay out his reading glasses, forcing him to set off on a tedious quest until he finally found them sitting atop a pile of laundry she hadn't folded yet, let alone ironed, even though he was in desperate need of his undershirts—she knows he freezes easily, especially when he sweats as much as he does. Or like when he discovers she put away the radio he wants to repair, and he doesn't even bother looking for it because he knows that compared to everything she is constantly putting away, sometimes in one spot, sometimes in another, this would be particularly tricky to find.

Today would have been the day. He can feel it. After confronting her about the pants, he would have set about calmly taking apart the radio, unbothered, as if he had all the time in the world, and he would have passed the entire afternoon that way, poking around with his screwdriver, getting worked up only when he was finished: why had he come home to find a note, and a ripped one at that, the kind you pass to someone who's already sitting on a train when you're in a hurry. A message scribbled out in a rush. *Arrive safe.* Or, *Be well.* And the person only just manages to reach it through the moving window, whereby the hands can no longer touch, are connected now only by the note, *Farewell.*

Imagining this makes him afraid: he could come home one day and she would be gone, but this time, it would be forever. Would he be able to tell right away? That it was for good? Maybe it would be evident in the way she had cleaned, like had happened to a colleague of his: One day he came home to find everything spotless, down to the very last wrinkle, the whole place brighter and happier than it had been in years. No dust. No crumbs. No hair. And he sat there in that cleanness and knew, even though he hadn't had the inkling beforehand: she wasn't coming back. She had even put fresh sheets on the beds. Beaten out the carpets. And on the walls, in the space where photos used to hang, were instead yellow-rimmed rectangles, and when he managed to recover somewhat, he papered over them with wallpaper, which, when he had had too much to drink, he liked to say was the most hideous thing he'd ever seen: a purple unicorn in front of a waterfall. *It just comes shooting down! With a roar*—slurring—*that devours every other noise.*

People had to keep topping off his drink, they did this again and again, until he mustered the courage to climb into a taxi and return to his silent home. But a lot of the time, he simply stayed in the city, spent the night if it was nice on a bench in the park, or booked himself a cheap hotel room if it was raining. Then when he turned up in the office the next morning, the first thing he did was go to the bathroom to shave. His face, when he emerged—no one would have suspected he would kill himself six months later—it was as smooth as a baby's—nor could they have guessed he would do so by winding a cable around his neck while he kneeled in front of the waterfall, as he explained in the letter they found after the fact, in his locker with his toothbrush and washcloth and razor, and in which he asked them to excuse the unsavory nature of his deed, thanked them in the PS for the time they spent listening to him, and for all those happy times they'd shared.

They wouldn't forget him, right?

Now, they hadn't had any children. And that makes a difference.

"Right?" he asks loudly into the silence. "So our situations can't be compared?"

No response.

He turns on the television. Lets it run as he looks for the radio; he'll find it somewhere—this house doesn't lose anything.

"It spits everything right back out again, isn't that right?"

The newscaster is talking about a level 4.2 earthquake that you could feel, but that hadn't caused any notable damage. This was followed by a listing off of lesser earthquakes, measurable but not perceptible, but he's barely listening. When he opens the closet under the stairs, a broom handle nearly falls on top of him, and he only just manages to dodge it. Why hadn't his wife hung it up on the mount put up expressly for this purpose? Another slip. He makes a mental note. And the cleaning supplies too. Doubled and tripled. He counts four glass cleaners, not a single one of which has been used, the safety locks are all still unopened, the windows sure could do with another wipe-down, you can't see outside anymore, he thinks, but, "Is that right? We have enough money lying around to throw at *glass cleaner*! And throw where, exactly? On the *windows*!" A grim joke that gives him a grim sort of pleasure, yes, he's on the verge of grinning, when in the same moment he senses his wife behind him, she must have slipped in through the back door, and who knows how long she was lurking there, waiting for him to almost—almost!—grin.

"Those were on sale," she said, "four for one."

And it takes him a second to register this, swallows, is the ground swaying a little? A chef's voice comes from the television: eggplants are rich in potassium, phosphorus, and B vitamins, they're great for lowering your blood pressure. His, on the other hand, is rising. He needs to find something to hold on to, the broom handle would be perfect, there we go. Now don't go losing your nerve. He thinks of the pants' pockets. The battle isn't over yet. There is still time. Stand your ground. Ask,

"You're back?" even though the answer is obvious. Wait for her "I am, as you can very well see." And then.

But she has already turned away from him, and he sees her from behind, hunched over, a grocery bag in each hand, disappearing into the kitchen. She disappears, simply disappears, without another word, and to him it feels, as he watches her go, as if she were about to dissolve before his eyes. An apparition. Or is it the hallway light that lends her silhouette a liquid quality? Even the bags seem to be dissolving, leeks towering out of them. He blinks.

"It's just an illusion, right?" But this is only a whisper.

The chef has begun to cook, with whatever it is spitting and sizzling. The audience oohs and aahs. Dolled-up housewives, all of them—he knows this without having to look, and he asks himself what he's doing there, in the closet under the stairs, he meant to look for something, meant to find something. Something that has gone missing. But what was it again? Right! The radio! He's happy when he is able to remember it again, as happy as he is about the refrigerator door, which he can hear being opened and closed again. In reality, nothing has happened at all.

CHAPTER TEN

As soon as he enters the kitchen—through the dividing curtain he fears he'll get trapped in every time even though he makes sure to push it back with both hands, never with just one, that would be careless—he can already sense, because of the way his wife is chopping the leeks, in small, precise little pieces, and in the process blowing a strand of hair out of her face, that it was wrong to come in here. He should have gone into the living room, lain down on the floor and taken a short nap, or at least pretended to. Lain there quietly, eyelids quivering, as if behind them one dream was chasing another.

He is good at that. He has had enough practice. And they fell for it constantly: "Psst, not so loud! Papa is sleeping!" They covered him up. Went around on tiptoes. Left him lying there like that for the rest of the day, without demanding or expecting anything of him except that he was asleep and therefore using the living room. When someone changed the channel, he would let out a groan, and it was quickly switched back: "Come on, you already know that will wake him up!"

And he relished this little bit of attention and the way they bestowed it upon him, their sleeping father, relished the scurrying of shadows and the fact that he could tell them apart, knew exactly who was who even with his eyes closed: that's his wife pushing a pillow behind his head, those are his children who are holding back a laugh for his sake. It was a spell that broke as soon as he began to stir, a magic circle surrounding them all in equal measure; *family* was the only word that came close to defining that spell, murmured in the wake-slumber of his un-dreamed dreams, as if it had climbed out from somewhere deep in his lungs, or deeper, from his stomach. A soft feeling in his mouth. And he could taste it. He ran his tongue along his teeth.

"You were out shopping?"

"Where else?"

His wife had packed the chopped leeks into a freezer bag. Next, aha, she set the ginger in front of her.

"And then?"

"What do you mean, 'then'?"

"Well," he glances at the clock above the cabinet, "you sure were gone awhile."

She stops chopping for a moment, as if to try to understand him better. He can see that her hands are trembling ever so slightly. And around her neck—or is he just imagining this?—is a tinge of red.

"Well, if you must know"—she is chopping again—"I was at the gym. They also offer dance classes. Ballet for seniors and that sort of thing. I . . . signed . . . up." More finely chopped words and the strands of hair, she needs to pin them back, they're always falling in her face.

He wants to take a hairpin and do it for her, help her, but he doesn't know how. Instead, he is staring at the ginger, which looks like a crippled foot, five toes, all there, but so bent they are useless. One foot, he thinks, that can't walk, or even limp, just gets in the way, what does a person even do with a foot like that? A foot that's only a source of frustration?

She says the first hour is free, "a trial hour." And the instructor, she says, her eyes on her workstation, "Yes, the teacher is a man," trained under so-and-so. So many names. He wonders where this is headed. An entire family tree of ballet teachers in tight pants and tiny shoes, but so be it. If she enjoys it, then she should have it. A hobby, something to keep her in shape, and she continues with a list of arguments for it to which there can be no objection, and as she is going down the list for him, he gets the impression she is dancing away in the dusty spotlight across a stage so huge that he gets lost on it, and he wants to follow her, capture her, but the curtain is there, and so heavy, and with people behind it who are coughing ever so slightly, along with a thick darkness.

Isn't she too old for that? That's his way of drawing her back to him. But she doesn't respond, continues coughing, next, aha, the spring onions. So he repeats himself, she probably didn't catch it.

"Aren't you too old for that?"

"Sure, maybe." A short pause. Then she smiles.

And he remembers the way she stood there, pressed against the door, conspicuously tall, even though he was at least a head taller than she was, he can still hear how she asks him, so polite, a girl from a good house, not to make any noise, her parents are already asleep, which at that point only made him want to make a racket, and the only reason he didn't was because touching her under her shirt wasn't enough, he wanted more, while she smiled at him the way she's doing now, so that he felt stupid, he is always the one to stumble while she . . . dances.

And now he's almost forgotten again. The radio. Where could she have hidden it? He needs it. Now. And he is in the process of making himself big and formidable—squaring his shoulders, his arms lifted slightly, a stance he wanted to save for the confrontation about his pants but got ahead of himself—when it catches his eye, it's stowed high up between broken rice cookers and party platters, and what he lost up there finally hits him, the radio, now it is suddenly *his,* it is certainly not a kitchen appliance, he says, trying to say it as kindly as possible, but his voice has taken on a life of its own, and he is startled by how rude it sounds. "What?" She stored it there temporarily because it was in her way? And if he wants to, he could get it down and put it in his room? If he wants to!

He climbs onto a chair and sees how filthy it is up here, years' accumulation of dust and grease on top of the cupboard, and he finds it lovely, really just lovely, that this was where she chose to stow his radio, where there is the most dirt—what was she thinking? Not a thing, apparently! You need a head to think after all! And he clutches it tightly, the poor thing, clutches it against his chest just before—how quickly it all happens—the chair begins to wobble, and he imagines he is already beginning to fall, down into the abyss, and in his panic, he's sure he'll break his neck, and then the radio slips and lands with a crack on the floor and instantly produces a terrible static.

"It's alive!" he cries.

Back on solid ground again, he bends over the chipped case and turns the dials, does this until the static turns into a squawk, then the distorted voice of a Frenchman, or is it music? He kneels so he can put his ear to the speaker.

"A waltz," he whispers. "The one from the movie!"

His wife, crouched beside him, nods without a word. And they listen, both of them do, listen carefully to the three-quarter tempo, which mingles with the other sounds in the house that all but eclipse it: the cooking show (the housewives are allowed to taste now), the dripping faucet, neighbors' voices (one is currently gargling), the distant wailing of an ambulance. All of it together creates a perfect harmony, and seems to belong together—his clearing of his throat when he finally stands up, her sniffing, which she blames on the onions.

And the way it all comes undone, in the next second already, when she asks him how things ended up at the doctor's, but he doesn't want to talk about that right now, not about the fact that nothing is the matter with him, but she keeps nagging, and so he promptly invents something with his heart, nothing bad, just something to keep an eye on. And he implores her not to worry for his sake, it's just a small thing, at which point she looks him directly in his eyes—when was the last time she did that?—and so he says it again, to remain in her gaze.

"Just a small thing."

CHAPTER ELEVEN

The rest of the day passes uneventfully. He put the radio back on top of the cabinet, not such a bad spot after all, he isn't forced to see it constantly and be reminded of when he almost went ballistic in the electronics store where he'd brought it over five months ago now, when they told him it wasn't worth repairing, that it would be cheaper to buy a new one, although there was only a handful left in stock, because, and this a little sympathetically: "They went out of style," but if he was still interested, they could check in the back.

Yes, he wanted them to do that.

They were out, of course. Should they place an order? A one-to-two-week turnaround? And then, without giving an answer, with a look intended to punish them, he stomped outside, hell-bent on repairing it himself, and to do it within one to two weeks, which to him seemed like an eternity, seven to fourteen long days, nights as well, any longer would become a joke if he didn't manage it. Determined, he went to his local library to browse the physics section for suitable material, unfortunately without success, at which point in the bookstore, where they were unable to help—"How very helpful, I'm so grateful!"— they suggested he look it up on the internet, might he be familiar with that? Yes, of course he's familiar, he isn't *that* old.

So that took up the first day. And by the second, he had slept so badly he couldn't find the energy to take any further action. He consoled himself with the words *long-term project*. They sounded hopeful. And in all honesty, not a single day goes by without him thinking, at least once, about how he will pull the radio down, take it very carefully apart, for one can never be too careful with such things, and how he would then sit there, in the glow of the lamp, which he set very close to him, marveling at the interior life revealed before him, all those cables and coils, he would just sit there in wonder, breathing deeply.

And then? This is the point he arrives at daily. And today is no different. He considers whether he should organize the records instead, but he can't decide, can't ever decide, how to best categorize them. Perhaps by era, he muses wearily. Meanwhile, the bonsai has died and needs to be composted, along with the soil. The pot as well, because without a plant, it serves no purpose. Come evening, he steps outside. The women fall silent, then pick up their conversation again, and their children whiz past him on their scooters and squint into the evening sun.

The moon appears low in the sky, it still has a ways to climb. And his house is the highest one, without a doubt. When he goes back inside, his mind wanders briefly to the homeless man. Might he also be heading home to his camp along the river? And might he feel as weary as he does? He tries to imitate his gait. Small and hunched. He can imitate it more easily than he would care to admit.

At dinner, the effects of his invented heart condition are re-vealed for the first time. His wife outdid herself. It's evident in the care she put into presentation, like the fried chicken, for example, served on lettuce leaves instead of the usual paper tow-els, and the cherry tomatoes carved into flowers, and when he reaches for the salt in the spot he would normally find it, he reaches into empty space, and she appears to have been wait-ing for that, and for him to get subsequently agitated, because she says, in a tone that's firm but also gentle, the way she would speak to a sick child: "Too much salt isn't good for you."

At which point, he stays agitated for just a moment longer, but with the pleasing sensation that a boundary has been set for him, and he feels as it closes in around him, a thick film on his skin, like the caress of a warm towel, and he gets a sudden chill. Could she top off his glass? A little more tea? He extends his mug. Rising steam. If he were to work the white Pomera-nian into the conversation now. She would be open to it. He can feel it. A dog would keep him up and moving, and would in turn also improve his daily walk, and well, why not? If it really means that much to him? But then he pictures the reality: Shiro wouldn't be half as smart as he hoped and would always be stepping on loose nails, and he'd be yippy on top of every-thing, and he imagines his disappointment when, after just three walks, they stop being enjoyable altogether, because Shiro stops every few corners, forcing him to have to bend over and pick up his little piles of poo. And the food! Who would haul that up the mountain? To say nothing of the vet bills he's heard about; those can be astronomical. About three hundred thou-sand yen is what cataract surgery would cost if he wants to keep

Shiro from going blind, which means at some point he would go blind, and it would be sad to see him lying there listless outside his little doghouse with his tail between his legs and his now-lackluster fur strewn all over the lawn. No. No dog. Even if his wife insists. At least not right now.

It's the same as with a third child. She wanted one for a long time, and he still remembers the way she used to harangue him in her silk nighties that appeared suddenly overnight from some drawer smelling of mothballs, and then how she gave up in the end, "at least for right now," and the nighties disappeared. He came across them in a box again just recently, covered in moth holes, and seeing the holes made him feel sorry he had been so stubborn. They could have handled one more. And the issue of space, which had been his main argument against it—there simply wasn't enough money for an extension—seemed trivial looking back now. It would have pushed them all closer together.

He doesn't need anything. Thanks. Actually, wait! If she would be so kind? The pockets!

"Oh dear." His wife claps a hand to her chest. "I completely forgot." And she goes to fetch her sewing basket. "I'll do it now!" He should take off his pants.

"What, you mean now?"

"What else would I mean?"

He hears her rummaging around in the closet under the stairs. It can't wait? No, better to just get it over with. She returns. He would prefer it to be later. But he doesn't say so.

"It's not that urgent," he says anyway.

"Don't be silly. The lamp. It's so bright in here."

He glances at the leftover cherry tomatoes. To get them to look like that certainly requires a great deal of finesse.

"Well." He stands up. "If I must."

Though he is personally of the opinion that she can take out the seams later, she put it off for all these weeks after all, and now she's turning it into a whole ordeal. Sometimes he has to wonder. *I mean, here! In the middle of the living room? Could she at least shut the curtains?* He is squirming. Plus, he has actually gotten used to not being able to put anything inside of them, and it's better this way, because his pockets would bulge if he stuck too much inside. And all this as he is undoing his belt, then his button, then his zipper—as he lets his pants down, he asks himself whether he shouldn't take off his socks too, because socks, at least to his mind, would highlight the nakedness of his legs, so he sighs and bends down to take them off as well, which he immediately regrets, because black lint has collected between his toes.

"Well, here you go, thank you very much! Are you happy now?"

And with that, he throws the pants at her feet, and while it was true that he meant to throw them unkindly, he only did so with one hand, not two, because that would have been too much. But his wife still grows strangely quiet, strangely motionless, and for a while, they stand there across from each other like that, him with his exposed, extremely exposed, legs, her staring blankly past him, as if there were someone standing behind him, perhaps the man he used to be, and she was trying hard to see him that way, the way he exists in her memory: leaving her at the door, giving her a dutiful kiss on the cheek, then spending almost an entire night below her window, promising her a life that would feel like dancing.

"I'm sorry," she says at last and holds up the pants.

The sound of crackling static as she smooths them out. Doesn't he want to have a seat? Red splotches on her curved neck. One quick snip and the thread comes loose. She pulls it out and rolls it into a tiny ball between her fingers.

CHAPTER TWELVE

I t's pitch-black when he turns off the light. But then, gradually, he can make out the contours of the furniture. There is his desk and computer; he completely forgot to look up what he'd planned to because of all his sweating. But he isn't sweating now, and for some reason it only seems necessary to look something up when he is, which means it's usually when he is out and about, which is probably the only reason he needs to in the first place: because there is no reason for him to be out and about in the first place. No direction, no destination in mind.

This is another one of those long chains of ideas that comes to him before bed as he watches the darkness thinning, as if pulled through a sieve, no longer obfuscating things but revealing them instead for what they are. Like his suitcase, for instance. He tripped over it again today. It was a goodbye present he received with a card, "Bon Voyage!" with all his colleagues' signatures. The colleagues he told all about his plans to fly to Paris with his wife as soon as he retired—which he still planned to do, for that matter.

There is a travel guide on his nightstand that he's thumbed through many times. And he knows exactly what dishes you can get where, knows the names of the hotels by heart. He's studied the map of the metro, along with local customs like how much to tip and that sort of thing. He will learn the most important phrases on the plane, he already bought a CD for precisely that purpose with examples to listen to, but he'll save all that for the second half of the journey, once they've spent the first half relaxing, leaning back in their seats, looking out the window, and enjoying the view. His slippers. Those he will miss. The little pillbox where he secretly stores a few poems he wrote years ago. The kind of poems someone might be embarrassed about but still can't bring themselves to throw away, because of that one line they agonized over. He can recite one from memory: "Sky Musings." And it goes like this—

—but he is already fast asleep, and his thoughts are only images that slip into the thickening darkness: a splintering sky, his wife chopping him up into small, precise little pieces. Trampling around atop stacks of papers filled with numbers and symbols, stomping them into the ground. Flapping through a fragrant jungle with the bird of paradise in heels and fearing, as he goes, that he'll get caught in the vines he grazes with his wings, while his wife is pelting him with balls of thread and he suddenly embraces her, naked for all the world to see, but she is not his wife at all but a crazy woman who packs him into his suitcase.

"You don't play family!" he shouts from inside.

But no one can hear him. His wife—he wakes up for a moment to see if he can hear her—is fast asleep.

PART
TWO

PART
TWO

CHAPTER THIRTEEN

Hello? Can I ask who's calling?"

"It's the cowboy from the graveyard."

"Pardon?"

"The one who was doing the swan."

"The swan?"

"You gave me your card."

He considers whether he should just hang up. It's embarrassing enough to have to explain, and now words are failing him, he wrote down a number of phrases on a sheet of paper. About the cowboy, about the swan. He had hoped those two would be enough.

"You are Mie, aren't you?" he asks.

"Mie who?"

And while he is struggling to maintain his composure, his phone pressed against his hot ear, she erupts in laughter, which now has him completely rattled.

"That made you sweat, didn't it? You thought I was being serious? But it's just like I said, by the second time, you know each other."

She knew he would have a hard time calling her, and she finds it cute, that's exactly what she says, *cute*, a word that seems completely ill-suited when applied to him. But a little fun never hurt anyone. And plus: "Rule number one: We don't remember the people we were close with yesterday. If we happen to run into each other again today, which is highly unlikely, we'll have forgotten them, like the speck of dust that trickled off our forehead while we slept. We have nothing to do with them." He should write this down. There must be a piece of paper nearby. "We'll talk more tomorrow." She gives the place and time. "You'll be there."

Not a question. A statement. His *but* is swallowed up by the dial tone; the word comes too late.

So off he goes. It's been a long time since he's taken the train anywhere, and never in the afternoon. So many open seats! He can sit wherever he likes. And yet he can't help but be drawn to the spot next to a young mother whose baby has just begun to scream at the top of its lungs. In turn, she moves a little farther away, placing between them a huge bag stuffed with diapers and bottles. A milky smell. He makes a face at the baby, and it stops crying. A toothless grin. Looks a little bit like an old man. He waves. But the mother acts like she doesn't care, shushes the child over and over, patting him rhythmically on the chest. When the baby squeals with delight, because now he's hiding behind his hands, then spreading his fingers and making faces at the baby, the mother turns him sideways, and the baby starts screaming all over again.

He lowers his hands. Backs away. Maybe he got too close to her and now, after being consumed all morning with her chest-patting, she has no desire to be near anyone who thinks they can do it better than she. Too bad. The baby raises its fists into the air, screaming. His face is blocked by the mother's back. He could tap her on the shoulder: "You don't need to worry. I'm not going to hurt you!" But she would probably interpret that as even more of an attack. It's really too bad. He looks at his hands. They're still quite useful.

A student with headphones is sitting diagonally from him. He's rocking gently from side to side, his eyes closed. If he were to open them, he wonders, what would he see? A mother and her baby and a man who doesn't belong with them? The train's rattling makes him nostalgic. This was the line he took to work day after day, and he often joked that it was his second home, so familiar were the doors and the alert when they opened and closed, the dangling straps and the smell of the books he dozed off to.

The passengers became familiar to him over time as well, he knew each of their stops. In addition to the bald man, there was the girl with Down's syndrome who used to chant along to the announcements, weaving in an additional greeting whenever someone new came aboard, which was the case at almost every stop: "Good morning! How are you? Pleased to meet you." They must teach that at school, and she seemed to enjoy it quite a bit, although she didn't seem to mind whether anyone answered or not, and practically no one did. Only once, it had been on his last day at work, had he worked up the courage— yes, he had to work up courage for a thing like that—and said hello, but the girl was completely disconcerted: all she did was stare at him, dumbfounded, and stayed silent for the rest of the ride. He hasn't seen her since. Does she still wear the pink frilly jacket? Only now does he realize how pretty she looked in it.

CHAPTER FOURTEEN

The agreed-upon meeting spot isn't that far from his old office, and it feels stranger and stranger the closer he gets to the building. So he takes a detour, not necessarily because he wants to explore but more so because he feels—it's that so-called gut feeling—that he no longer has a right to walk down this street leading to the office, and according to the TV program, it's important to follow your gut. It relays messages from deep inside of you and transports them to the surface to get your attention. People who suppress them often suffer from stomach ulcers.

He feels that this street belongs to the others now, and he needs to go around the back of the building, not the front, to keep from being spotted. How did this whole area, once so familiar, turn into what feels like foreign territory overnight? He feels like an intruder now, and you can tell by his walk, his darting eyes, that he has no business being here. He ducks. The man up ahead looks familiar.

Quick, cross the street! Switch sides! Looking at his phone, whose contract he wants to cancel soon because nobody calls him anyway and because he only really uses it for golf, but carries it around regardless because it gives him a sense of security to have it at the ready. When you look at your cell phone, you appear busy, and if you're busy, you don't call attention to yourself. His outfit, though. He should have chosen a proper shirt after all—anything but this new one that's only pretending to be a shirt.

At the shop where he bought it and the jacket, they said it was the ideal transitional shirt, a cross between the classic office shirt and a slightly more fitted casual shirt, although, they said, with a sideways glance at his gray temples, it was definitely more on the classic side. You don't wear it with a tie. No. Or jeans, either. The saleswoman thought it highlighted the experience radiating from him, which left him with a positive impression of her. As if her opinion mattered. A woman in her midforties who clearly didn't have much going on—two, three children, no husband, five jobs. He thought he detected a weariness in her voice, like the kind that came over him when he had to think about *tomorrow,* and despite her attentiveness— she offered to find him a matching cardigan because cardigans were all the rage now, people wore them with or without a shirt underneath—she seemed out of place to him. She should go home, draw a hot bath, and paint her nails.

He bought everything she foisted upon him, even the cardigan, though the pattern made him sick, checkered yellow and apricot, but then again, what did he know? Maybe she'll get points for it and a ribbon at the end of the year? Really, he just wanted to get out of there. Back into the fresh spring air. That had been on his first day of retirement, the day after he'd said hello to the girl on the train. Both incidents seemed connected somehow. A gut feeling. He's a good ways past the office now.

CAFÉ FRANÇAIS is printed on the piece of paper he pulled out of his pocket. His wife cut them open. And although it's

only been two days, it seems so long ago now, a lot further than
everything else that happened just before it.

She is already waiting for him. He spots her at a table in the
middle of the room. A high-cut top, flats, hair combed severely
back. Not the same Mie who stepped out of the tree's shadow
to clap for him. Instead, she introduces herself: "Today, I am
Satoko." An aunt who needs to be on her way very soon. But
they can get through a lot in twenty minutes, if he would please
just give her his full attention. She'll do the rest—the talking,
she means. A kind of audition. Satoko is a chatty aunt.

   "She only ever talks about herself, and in long, rambling
sentences that don't make any sense, so the person she's talking at has nothing to latch onto, a habit left over from wartime,
when you needed to say something in exchange for every kernel
of rice you ate, and whoever couldn't do it was killed—oh, it's a
joke! I'm not trying to pretend I'm a ninety-year-old!—but she
got that from her mother, who got it from her mother, which is
all to say: she got it from back when people . . . Well, I already
addressed that. Rule number two: We insert ourselves into the
network of relationships, if necessary, as far back as the mother's
mother's mother. We find the weak spots and make them our
own, because we believe every family has at least one weak spot,
and that weak spot exists in each member of the family. Without that"—she glances quickly at her watch—"we wouldn't be
human beings, just actors." The bartender brings over the tea.
"You drink tea, right? I took the liberty of ordering for you, and
black with lemon seemed right to me, no idea why, but it had

to have something acidic and something dark. I have kind of an animal instinct for that sort of thing. Take the shirt you're wearing, for instance. Let me guess. Your wife picked it out for you? No? But it looks good on you! It does! The light pink looks good with your complexion. I wouldn't have thought it was you. But you are married, yes? No matter. To get back to my point: we are nothing without our family, and what's more, we are nothing without their weak spots, which have shaped us for generations. Please write that down. Here, on the napkin. You'll need that when I send you on your way.

"All right, now look, there was just a request, something easy, truly. I promise. Something for beginners. Your grandson— his mother—which means, your daughter—booked you as a grandfather. I recorded the details for you on a tape—a little outdated, but you don't mind, do you? It saves us both a lot of time."

And with that, she hands him a Dictaphone along with a thick envelope, checks the time, takes a sip of water, stands partway up, and then sits right back down again. "Too quick?" She laughs. "That's how it goes. You'll have to get used to it." And with a sense of triumph, which he's already seen once before somewhere, on someone else's face, a triumph that feasts on his own astonishment: "You're hired! Congratulations. You passed the entrance exam with flying colors. I mean, your dance last time at the cemetery. That was enough for me. The way you transformed from a monkey to a swan and then from swan to human! No one will be able to top that anytime soon, Mr Katō!"

"Mr Katō?"

"Oh yes, your name! That's what you're called! God, you're slow. By the way, I've already paid for the tea, it's on the agency. One more thing: you have to work on your smile. Nobody believes you when you smile. The problem—you remember?—is with your body. It doesn't smile with you. Please write that down. Rule number three: When we get up in the morning, regardless of how bad we might be feeling, we get ourselves in front of a mirror, stick our arms up high—like this—and try to smile with our whole body. It's pointless if it's just your mouth doing it. Even your little toe should be smiling. Right now you're grinning! That is a subtle, subtle difference: anyone can grin. Not everyone can really smile. And I'll leave you with that little bit of wisdom. Good luck!"

Where is her purse, the one with the rhinestones? One last question to keep her here, because his little toe is telling him he doesn't want to let her go.

"Satako doesn't sparkle," she replies.

And before he can even get to it, the last question—what is her real name?—she has disappeared. He watches her hurrying toward the underground station through the glass door, and he tries to follow her with his gaze for as long as he can, her little head with the bun he didn't notice when she was facing him.

Only once she is underground, lost in the sea of larger heads, does he murmur, not audible to anyone but himself, "I would have preferred coffee." Black, no milk, no sugar.

CHAPTER FIFTEEN

You? Here? But that's not possible!"

Just as he's leaving, someone reaches for his shoulder, making him jump. The touch is so light he can hardly feel it, but it has a distinct smell—what is it, he wonders—and when he turns around, it hits him: a mix of camphor and menthol.

"It can't be!" He is happy to see him. "Fujimoto, old boy!"

And he is surprised by his happiness, but what's more, he is surprised that the joy he feels is real and that it arrived without him having to try to get himself to feel it. On his way back, he took an even bigger detour around the office, hugging the walls, hoping not to run into anyone. And here was the person he had least expected: *Mr Medicine Man.* A nickname that stuck to him just like the ointments he concocted, a hobby that primarily served his virility, which he told everyone about—that the essential oils he sourced from China (well, not directly from China, but from Chinatown) entered the body through the skin and that inside, he was only twenty, especially down there, thanks to their potency. They could feel free to ask his wife, she would confirm it. But the hump. Well, there is no cure for that. He got it from so much sitting—"modern man's cross to die on," as he put it.

And there was in fact something crucified about him: the

way he always seemed to be suffering, sometimes in one spot, other times another, constantly rubbing himself with his ointments, so that you could smell him from afar. All of them secret recipes he worked on at home in the laboratory set up specifically for this purpose, secrets that he revealed to them after three rounds of beer and in fact had nothing particularly mysterious about them, instead they induced yawning meant to change the subject, which he was sensitive about. Because that is precisely what's wrong with the world. That no one has the patience to stay on one topic anymore. People just jump from one to the next and miss out on the present. One of his favorite phrases—only someone who is in the present can heal—which no doubt came from that life-help talk show, they said the same kinds of things, even though he regretted watching them—it's all a sham, he said, the falsehoods they're peddling as truths on those talk shows.

In short: Mr Medicine Man was exhausting. But just seeing him standing here in front of him, skinny and hunched over as he is, gives him a real pleasure.

"It's been so long! How is work?"

And he asks after the colleagues. He is curious to know whether the seating arrangement has stayed the same, is everyone in the same spot, who took over his desk, ah, the short guy, and who was promoted, ah, the fat guy, and the longer they talk about it, the more important it becomes—who is sitting where and at which table—as if it said something about the state of things and he still had some say in it all. Is the coffee machine still that old one? You had to hit it; otherwise, you wouldn't get your change. Had the cleaning lady, the one without a nose, straightened her teeth? It was so creepy running into her at night when you were working overtime. What, she isn't there anymore? Fired? And more to that end, until suddenly the other asks him whether he's enjoying it, retirement? And how had Paris been?

"Lovely," he says, and it is too late to take it back. "We thought the Louvre was the best part."

"The Louvre, you say?"

"Yes, the Louvre."

Uttered three times, the word deformed tonally, it sounded ludicrous coming out of his lips. And the fourth time did not make it any better: In "the Louvre," they saw the *Mona Lisa*. Unbelievable, how small it is. You imagine it so much bigger in your mind. But her smile! How did the tour guide describe it? It seemed to lift off the wood so daintily and gently. A true masterwork. He puts his hands in his pockets. A sense of shame, but cockiness at the same time: he can do this, come up with lies like this. His heart doesn't even skip a beat. At least not in a way that would stop him from moving on to the delicious food next: in the Printemps restaurant, not far from the Gare de Lyon, you get excellent beef served with excellent wine, not expensive at all, the whole menu, including dessert, would not have cost them more than this-and-this-much; unfortunately, he couldn't remember the exact price, but every bite was worth it.

"Sounds amazing," says Fujimoto, looking him directly in the eyes. He repeats himself: "Just amazing."

Does he know how Itō's doing? He hurries to change the topic. No, and don't shy away, he wants to hear more, and besides, "Who cares about Itō? Compared to Paris!" They should meet up again soon. He would like to hear more about it, "and from you." And he conjures a little tin out of his sleeve, a trick he used to perform for them all the time.

"Voilà! This is for you!" An ointment. "Works wonders on whatever ails you: Sniffles. Sleeplessness. Dizziness." He'd had it with him this whole time. "And now I know why: for this very moment! I mean, it can't be coincidence. I just left the office after being made to look like a complete fool by the boss, and now here you are telling me about the Louvre. You see? About the Louvre! So now I'm asking myself what I'm really doing here. It's fate! I can finally see things clearly.

"Somewhere in the world there is a *Mona Lisa,* good food, good wine, and I can hold out, just two hundred and fifty-eight days, and then: Poof! Gone! Far away! I'll send you a postcard!"

He thanks him for the healing that's been done, he has a sense of perspective again, which will help him return to his desk with some dignity. When they say goodbye, he puts his hand on his shoulder again.

"I do mean it, let's get together again soon!" Adding, with a stress so light it's hardly noticeable, "You did it right!"

A postcard. Of course! He would have sent them one if he really had gone to Paris. And souvenirs. Those too. After his colleagues bought him that suitcase specifically for traveling. Beginner's mistake. What would Mie have to say about this? Probably (he can hear her laughing) that "we don't lie to falsify the truth, but in order to make it right." He believes he knows what she would say. The scent of camphor sticks to his shirt, and he tries to wipe it away, but it stays. A whiff of guilt. But Fujimoto didn't want it any other way. And besides: What actually is real, he asks himself, and what isn't? There is no fence separating one from the other. And if there were, then there are loopholes so big you can climb through, no problem, without getting caught on a stray wire.

On the other side is the very same soil, a little damp, but not so damp that you'll get stuck. You don't leave any prints behind. It only gets slippery the further you go. But as long as he stays close to the fence, he won't slip. He can come back anytime he wants. In a way, he did go to Paris. In a way, his heart does skip. Both are true somehow—he is setting things right. And he boards the train for home, and as soon as he sits down, he lets his head droop as if of its own accord. A movement that calms him, doesn't require him to think.

And yet now and again, when the train starts to sway, he can't help but think: whether the cleaning lady, who in truth he never found creepy, only said so because it belonged to his and Fujimoto's common language—which is still the case, he thinks weakly—whether she doesn't notice her missing nose anymore when she looks in the mirror in the morning, because after all, it's normal to her not to have one; instead maybe she looks at her hair—it looks nice today, she might say, turning coyly to the side, pursing her lips in a self-satisfied smile over her crooked teeth? Even as he dozes off, she appears before him: her hands planted defiantly on her hips. What does she want, he wonders, his head bobbing.

All around him, everyone is sitting in the same position.

CHAPTER SIXTEEN

I was in the city."

"Oh?" His wife is in the middle of scrubbing the front steps. The moss is being stubborn, she pants. Stubborner than last year, even. "Or maybe it's me who's being stubborn?" She says this quietly to herself. And to him: "Careful! It's slippery!"

"I know, I know."

She could have waited for him to do it. It's on his list after all, not hers.

"Let me try."

But she doesn't back down. "I can do it." She can see he's tired.

"Certainly not!"

He opens his eyes wide. And could she maybe stop for a second to ask him how he's feeling? He picked up that sentence somewhere, along with the gesture he makes, borrowed, anyway: turning away, but only partially, so that he could be held back in the event she were to hold him back, and only then would he turn away completely. But she keeps scrubbing, doesn't pay him any more attention. And he looks at her arms, her muscles bulging with every scrub.

Don't bother, then, he thinks, and he reminds himself that this is reality, the only one there is. And there is no script to go along with it. No instructions: *Now go into the house. Fast. Slam the door behind you.* He does it anyway. No camera panning. The lens stays focused on him in a long shot. He kicks off his shoes. Considers briefly whether he should throw them into the corner. But then he sets them down neatly, the heels side by side.

He goes up the stairs to his room. Soft scrubbing noises come through the window. He tries to ignore it, which takes a lot of effort. Then he pulls the Dictaphone out of his pocket. How baggy his pocket's gotten already. He holds the device at a distance so he can make out the buttons. Everything is so tiny, like it's made for children's hands.

"Damn it!" he swears, pressing Pause multiple times. Why isn't this working? Then finally he hits Play.

"So! Where did we last leave off? Oh yes, on the fact that you need to work on your smile. Truly. You can't keep putting it off. It would be too sad if you were to die before you get to it, just imagine that for a second. It would mean that on your deathbed, people would say you were a good person, just a shame they hadn't recognized it earlier, when you were still alive. You see. I'm good at planning ahead. Nothing should be left to chance, it's the worst possible partner for stand-ins like us—that's what we call ourselves. We step in where we're needed and replace the actual actor, because yes, even the person we're playing is performing most of the time, which makes them an actor. It's true, there are people who aren't themselves even in sleep. Scary, right?

"But that's just the intro, now *[Mie clears her throat]* for the main part: The boy's name is Jordan. You heard me correctly. His father is an American, more specifically: African American, which only plays a role insofar as it's the reason why his grandfather, his real one, doesn't want to see him. Half-American, and on top of that, he has kinky hair. His grandfather never forgave him for being born. And that's about it. Please push the Stop button now and take a look at the photos. They're in the envelope I gave you. You'll find the Stop button on the right next to the Play button, it's marked with a black square *[a pause, long enough for him to find it]*."

Stop. Ten photos. There's a boy in them, just as she described: a little too delicate-looking for his taste, he prefers the stronger ones, but oh well, he is his grandson and perhaps he'll still grow a bit, one can hope. A photo shows him with his mother, they are nestled together in a tent on the beach, and you can see that they are exhausted from a lot of sun, their feet are pushed into the sand. He traces over the scene with his finger, a gesture he didn't borrow from anyone, and he doesn't know why he does it, he just has to touch them, it's the way they're sitting there, defenseless despite the tarp over their heads.

They resemble each other, even in the way they're eating their watermelon. The leftover rinds are familiar, all gnawed clean. A yellow dinghy in the background. They weighted it down with rocks so it won't fly away.

Play: "Adorable! Don't you think? The mother's name is Rumi. She is thirty-five, single mother, her boyfriend—excuse me, ex-boyfriend—moved back to the States while she was still pregnant. She works as a nurse. Please look at her again."

Stop. A portrait. Rumi isn't smiling. Still, she radiates a certain warmth. And it's not necessarily coming from her eyes—where, then?—but instead—can that be?—from every pore of her skin. He considers her face. An age spot here and there. Smile lines, worry lines. A birthmark on her chin, almost heart-shaped. Not beautiful, for that she lacks a certain symmetry, but it is precisely that crookedness—everything slightly askew, one nostril seems bigger than the other—which gives her a certain charm and makes her likable straightaway. A buddy. She is someone who would be fun to grab a drink with.

Play: "Now back to you! So, Rumi's father. A Mr Katō Ryusuke, sixty-five, widowed, former mayor of the little town called N, in case you know it, an insignificant provincial town where he has himself probably remained an important figure to this day. An unsullied reputation as you can imagine, quite an upstanding citizen. The only blemish: the boy. He is supposed to stay out of his sight.

"According to Rumi, he blames him for the death of his wife, who died of a stroke shortly after her grandson was born. She had written Rumi a letter saying how much she was looking forward to holding Jordan—what a lovely name that was—and sent along onesies and toys, with the PS: 'Not a word to your father. You know what he's like.' When things had calmed down again, she would come and see her—very soon, she hoped. Does she need any money?"

Stop. He takes a deep breath. Tears were pricking his eyes, catching him off guard. Why is he crying now, he wonders, he would very much like to rip open the window and call down to his wife to just leave it, the scrubbing. The moss would only come back next year. How very lonely. How pointless. He glances at the slippers, whose soles are already worn through in some places. Not even the homeless man would want them anymore. But that's not something to cry over. One more deep breath. He rubs his face. Don't let the tears run. Blink.

And play: "Now for your assignment, Mr Katō. Like I said, this shouldn't be anything too difficult. You should stop over for tea for three or four hours, depending on how Jordan responds to you, talk to him a bit, ask him how he's doing, how school is going, in short: Make him feel like he has someone else besides his mother who cares about him. Play some catch. You can play catch, can't you? Admire his new bike. Watch him do a headstand and say, 'Wow, you're so good at that!' Stuff like that, nothing too exciting.

"Under no circumstances should you give the impression that you want to make amends. Rumi would like [*she clears her throat again*] for you to show that you're human. That's very important to her. And *human,* I quote, for them means being *as normal as possible.* Which means behaving like someone who's been there the whole time, although I tried to make her understand that that's not so easy to do, because after all, Jordan is at an age where he can already see through a lot. But what can you do? She's got it in her head that you've really never been away. She told the boy that—and this part is true, at least—you are a busy man way up north, which sounds like Santa Claus, if you ask me, but he seems to believe it, which is the whole point! He is supposed to believe in you the same way he would in someone who doesn't actually exist! He always gets a little package from you on his birthday. She picks it out in a department store and has it shipped to her home. The last gift was a globe. If you could please remember that? You gave it to him so that he would know—it's a big world out there."

CHAPTER SEVENTEEN

For five days, he has been getting up and going to stand in front of the mirror, regardless of how badly he feels, sticking his arms up high in the air and attempting to smile with his whole body. But he can't do it, doesn't even come close. It's still just his mouth smiling, not his eyes, not his heart, never mind his little toes. And he wants to throw it away, all of it, because he's just wasting his time. He could be fixing his radio instead. But then his wife asks him at dinner what's the matter with him, he looks so different.

"Different how?" he asks in response.

To which she pokes around helplessly on her plate.

"I don't know. Just different. As if you're on vacation, on a ship, and you're walking around the deck under an umbrella, watching the waves. Something like that. Like you're in first class."

That was the best comparison she could come up with. And he notices the way she is looking at him, peeking at him, and the way she seems to be searching for the right word, it's on the tip of her tongue, to describe how "different" he looks. And he is searching for a word as well, just as unsuccessfully, to describe the "peace" that has come over them.

Ever since he's been working on his smile, there has hardly

been cause to argue. The roof, yes! He still thinks he needs to have it checked. She, on the other hand, thinks it's a waste of money, they have time before it starts raining on their heads. But other than that, they've been getting along rather well. He eats what she puts in front of him, reaches for the salt just for the fun of it, which makes her laugh a little because he acts like the saltshaker is still there and pretends to salt his food with it, and he laughs a little too, then they continue to eat, making little remarks about whatever is on TV. As she washes the dishes, he thinks of Rumi and how she wishes her son could have a scene like this: nothing too exciting. Plates clattering.

He leans back in his chair. On the news, they're talking about a distant war. Some troops that landed somewhere, and how grisly it is, but at the same time a consolation: he has peace in his house at least. At least he would if the plates weren't clattering like that. He was the one who'd been against having a door there, he just wanted a curtain. He found it cozy that instead of being divided, the kitchen and living room were essentially combined into one *joint* room. Because together, they make up the heart of the home.

And he finds it cozy even today: propping his feet up to the sound of running water, then waiting for her to turn it off when she's through. Next she'll bring him a beer, and he doesn't need to say thank you, because it is understood; he knows exactly how it tastes before he even brings it to his lips, slightly bitter, slightly sweet, could be a little colder.

"Look at the moon!" says his wife and points out the window.

And for a whole moment, they're gazing together at the

white, glowing crescent, which always, every single time, makes them stop and stare in wonder.

"Beautiful!" they say, almost at the same time.

He can pick her immediately out of the crowd surging onto the platform. Rumi is wearing a cap with an American flag. Her father would have taken it as a provocation, or maybe she would not have put it on to begin with, would have stood there facing him obediently with her head bowed, wouldn't have been able to get herself to look him directly in the eye. There. *What's wrong with it?* she would have thought, and he allows her the freedom she needs to be able to say: *This is who I am, take it or leave it. He, the father, has no power over me.*

The boy is hiding behind a pillar a little ways away. He peers around it shyly, on the one hand curious, on the other reluctant to reveal his hiding spot. When she calls him: "Jordan! Come here and say hello!" he runs off toward the exit. Stops briefly at the steps to look back at them. Then storms all the way to the top.

"You'll have to excuse him." Rumi comes to his defense. "He's going through a phase. You know what I mean, some pre-pubescent thing. But he is looking forward to this. Very much! He's been talking about it all morning, about everything he wants to do with you."

"No problem at all," he says. And to show he understands: "I was exactly the same at that age." It will pass in time. "Here, all the way from home!"

He extends a box of milk cookies that had been a real pain

to find. Five long days spent smiling and researching where you could find them, precisely this kind of milk cookie, and although this hadn't been in Mie's instructions, it felt important to bring something sweet, it had to be something sweet. *Our cows produce the best milk in the country,* he wanted to add when he handed it to her, because he is the former mayor of the town of N after all, but then he decides it would be silly, because she has accepted the box so tenderly, as if it contained God only knows what precious objects, and as she presses it to her cheek, she slips for a moment, just briefly, back into a childish dialect.

"Oh, thank you!" she says. "I've missed these so much!" And, glancing up the steps, "Let's go home."

A choice of words that binds him to her. *Home.*

Jordan has taken a seat on the top step, and when he spots her, he jumps up and darts off again. He hides the whole way home, sometimes behind a power pole, sometimes behind a blooming azalea bush, and as soon as they're about to catch up to him, he's off again. A game that soon takes on a life of its own, and he plays along, wondering in a loud voice where he could possibly be, that rascal, then, completely surprised, exclaiming: "Oh, there he is!" To which all three have to laugh, finally together again after so many years apart, but they don't waste any time thinking about that, not on this bright blue day that feels a little bit like a holiday. At some point, Jordan stops. He waits until they catch up, and then they continue as a trio.

"You *must* show me your new bike. I heard you cleaned it specially for me? Is that really true? And you even oiled the chain? All by yourself?"

The boy nods, proud. No one showed him how, but it wasn't even that hard.

"That's good! You're becoming a man!"

His hand is resting gently on his head. His kinky hair feels like coiled thread. If he wants, he could teach him how to patch a tire in case he ever got a flat. Or how about? They could use their finger to travel around the world? He had sent him a globe for his birthday after all. Did he like it? Jordan blinks up at him. And for a split second, he believes he can read a vague distrust, he sees it flare up, a flash in the pan that goes out just as quickly as it appeared. Or was he only imagining it? They continue walking. Every now and again, they brush up against each other. And he feels the delicateness of the small body beside him, feels big and rough in comparison. The warm little hand that slips into his when they're nearly at the front door—he wishes they hadn't arrived yet, that they would keep walking like this forever. A tickle in his toes. He smiles.

CHAPTER EIGHTEEN

Their home is a one-bedroom. Plainly decorated, but not impoverished by any means. Watercolors are hung up on the wall. In her free time, which is a rare commodity these days (Rumi says this without bitterness), she has taken up painting. He: "You were always good at that." She: "I got it from Mom." And while they drink their tea and nibble on their milk cookies, they remember "Mom," which isn't hard for him, because she sprinkles crumbs along the way, so all he has to do is follow them, through a sadness he knows intimately himself, and certain things occur to him, long-forgotten things, for instance, how devoted she was to her garden, her favorite flowers were hydrangeas, and oh, how fragrant it had been in summer when you leaned out the window in the morning, and there she was, already up and waving cheerfully with the watering can in one hand and scissors in the other, a sight that always gave him a pang, she looked so fragile next to the flowers' opulence. Or how good of a cook she was.

"Mm-hmm," he munched, "the best scrambled eggs in the world!" You would think there isn't an art to it, but to Jordan, who was listening attentively: "There's a certain finesse to preparing them so that the tongue carries the taste straight to the heart, and you're spoiled forever, you can't eat anyone else's scrambled eggs ever again." Does he know what the most important ingredient of all was? "No, not the eggs, but—" He gets goose bumps when he whispers it and feels a twinge of embarrassment, but it's exactly this embarrassment that sends a pleasant shiver down his spine: "Love." A word best spoken quietly, or else it loses—his hairs stand up again—its magic.

"Love," Jordan whispers back.

And all of it seems to transform into something tangible before them: the set table with the now-eaten milk biscuits—there is one left. The teapot that is no longer steaming. The yellow roses in the vase.

"If Mother were with us now"—he looks thoughtfully at the single petal that is about to fall—"she would be so glad we are all together. But who knows? Maybe she's closer than we think."

Whereby he is seized with an emotion that he is no longer pretending to feel, and he has to excuse himself, he is a weepy person. It probably has something to do with getting older. The littlest things make him sentimental these days.

"But, Papa"—Rumi passes him a tissue—"you don't have to apologize. It's only natural that you miss her, even after six years, grief never goes away, not overnight. And because she passed so suddenly, her death will have a lasting effect. Sometimes I think she's dying over and over again."

"You can't think like that." Now it's he who's comforting her: "She lives on. Think of it that way. She lives on in you and Jordan."

Jordan has meanwhile rolled into a ball and is meowing like a cat.

"Now look what we have here, a little cat." And he tickles his belly until he laughs and stretches out his claws.

"No tickling! Please, no!" And when he stops: "Again! Again!"

"Not so wild," Rumi warns.

"Oh, he's fine! A boy should be allowed to run amok once in a while."

"Then please do it outside!" She shoos them out the door and seems relieved but worried at the same time, he can see it in the way she watches them go. "Have fun," she calls.

And they most certainly would.

"And? Did you?" Sitting across from each other in the Café Français the next day, Mie is in no hurry to go anywhere, and he wonders if she is herself today, hair down to her shoulders, no makeup, or at least not enough for it to be noticeable—however women manage to make it look like that—and in a flowy wrap that showcases her figure all the more by hiding it, even if he did prefer the skintight top.

"Oh, we did indeed! This Jordan"—he leans back in his chair—"is a fine specimen of a boy."

He would have loved to have a son like that. And he thinks of his own, already grown, and his disappointment after taking a Sunday afternoon off to play catch with him, but his son preferred to stay on the couch with a book under his nose and a bag of chips next to him that crinkled every time he reached inside, which induced a blinding rage, not at him but instead at his wife, at what a pansy she had raised him to be, and then at his son anyway, at the way he was sitting there with his greasy fingers when all he wanted was to play catch just once, just this once—was that too much to ask?

"A fine specimen, you say?"

"Certainly a good catcher, we played baseball in the park, and as more and more of his friends started to show up, we had enough to form a legitimate team. The time flew by so that we really had to hurry to make it back home on time. Then after that, he showed me his bike, and I admired it. It was bright red with a bell, but—" Here he balked.

"Not that exciting, I hope, Mr Katō!" And because she thought he lost his train of thought: "So to repeat: He showed you his bicycle. You admired it. And then?"

"He started to cry."

He didn't notice at first, but as he was tightening the handlebars, raising the seat a little higher, it gradually became more and more quiet behind him.

"And that, even though he had just been chattering away, and then I turned around and saw that snot was running from his nose, he was—as you would put it—sobbing with his whole body, but without making a single sound. And it lasted awhile. But then."

"Then?"

"He said some things that I think his mother should be made aware of. Things that indicate, no, not just indicate, that he and his grandfather . . ."

"If you would please"—she taps on the table with her pointer finger for emphasis—"get to the point! I don't want to be here forever. I only have two hours before I am Saya, a hippie girl."

She spares him the details. So this isn't her, he thinks, and for some reason feels happy about this. "That he and his grandfather . . . ?" she prods him.

"Had met before. An older man, he said. He was short and fat. And he waited for him after school and walked with him for a stretch. Hadn't he been afraid? Only a little, but he was very friendly, asked him how his mother was doing, if she had to work a lot. Which he said she did, and explained that he spent most of his time home alone, at which point the man gave him a key chain. Which he asked him to keep between them, a secret, but he had it with him and showed it to me, a chain with the town of N's coat of arms, with his name engraved underneath it: *Katō Ryusuke, Mayor,* which of course he, the six-year-old, can't read, apart from the last name perhaps. Either way, he got the impression that somehow this old man had something to do with him, which made him feel sorry for me, he said, "because I like you a lot," but he felt even sorrier for his mother, who so seldom seemed to be in such a good mood. Could he still keep the globe anyway? And all that between sobs, while I was busy checking the tire—"

"You were doing *what*?"

"Checking the tire pressure. That calmed him down. I said, 'This needs a little more air.' Does he know how to do that? Of course he knows how to do it. So he knelt to open the valves. I was beside him. With the pump. And by the time we were done—less than five minutes—he was laughing again."

"Very insightful." Mie shakes her head.

"It was," he decides. "But if I may, and please excuse me, beginner's question. Should we not tell the mother?"

"Absolutely not! This is the sort of thing you need to clear up on your own. You did your part, and up until the milk cookies—no gifts like that in the future, not unless I say so—and apart from the hour longer that you stayed—we don't stay longer unless it's a wedding or funeral—you did great. Bravo!"

She claps.

The people at the next table exchange questioning glances. But Mie ignores them. She makes a point to speak louder.

"Next, you're a husband. And at that, one that doesn't say anything. Here's the tape." He should destroy the other one. "Hit it once, and then it's broken! One advantage to it being so old-fashioned."

"No rules today?"

"Not today. Saya, the hippie girl, I'll tell you this much, she can't stand rules."

And they spoke awhile longer about this and that, like how as a stand-in you should be as flexible as possible, for example, but they just kept looping back to the grandfather: Why had he given his grandson a key chain with his name on it but then been unable to face his daughter? Maybe, this was his theory, because he hoped she would happen to find it in Jordan's pocket when she was doing the laundry? Or maybe, Mie's theory, he hadn't planned to, just wanted to walk a little ways with the boy, and had come up with the idea only then, without really wanting to, of giving him something of himself, which he now bitterly regrets, because it exposes his shortcomings?

"I mean, who knows? How often had he stood there before that? In front of the school, in front of her apartment? And how often had he held himself back? These are all questions we will never have the answers to, or that there are at least only cheesy answers for."

"So no happily ever after?"

"It's possible. But"—she looks out at the street—"that would be too simple, wouldn't it?" Wouldn't all these people be happy, then? Herself included? "Which they definitely aren't?"

"What? You aren't, either?"

"Well, Saya might be, sure! But she has her own story too, and it comes back to her when she's strolling barefoot through the prairie, stoned out of her mind, talking to rocks and birds—it comes back to her before she's sober again. The foundation of happiness, as I explained to you, is in truth just shaky ground, and we might be able to balance, some better than others, but that doesn't change the fact that it could go out from under us at any point, and just knowing that is all we can do, knowing that both feet are poised at the edge of the precipice."

"Better hold on tight, then," he wants to say and give her a little wink along with it, but Mie's face has frozen into a mask, and he is afraid it will crack if he takes his eyes off it for even just a moment.

"Tired?"

"Not even a question."

And he takes her hand, which is lying lifelessly on the table, and gives it a little squeeze before she pulls it away. He feels the cold in her fingers and the way it lingers on his skin, feels it long after she rebukes him, joking: what would his wife say, he's married after all. He remembers her like someone he lost sight of an eternity ago and hasn't seen since. It's true, she exists. But as for what she would say? Probably that he . . . Well, what? He doesn't know.

CHAPTER NINETEEN

Dancing is good for her, his wife says. She's been learning a lot, by which she means "relearning." And it's so interesting, the way the body—she moves in front of him—stored it all.

"And after almost forty years! Interesting, isn't it? How it was able to remember, as if it has been lying dormant inside me the whole time and is now finally waking back up."

"What?"

"Dancing!"

And all she has to do is surrender to it, her body, and how it feels, so that dancing can find its way back to the surface, which she finds very interesting. *Dancing* three times, *interesting* three times. He counted. And next? Of course, the instructor! Which makes him realize that she is always talking about the instructor, but without ever saying his name, and by doing so, she puts him on a kind of pedestal, ascribing to him an almost superhuman power. He is just incredible, she says. He pulls out everything that's inside of her.

"And the way he does it! He's so sensitive and precise when he gives instructions. A real artist," she says, and after a pause, "It's too bad for him. I mean, too bad that this was where he ended up. He should really be somewhere else completely."

"And where would that be?"

"Somewhere where he can thrive! It's a waste of talent to be teaching a group of women over fifty in a suburb like this. Women who, sure, all have dance experience, but who also have, because of marriage and children . . ." Her voice trails off.

What she means is: women who have fallen out of practice. Does he see it that way too? The past few days, she's seemed to find it important to ask him his opinion. And what should he say? That he considers this dancing business (in contrast to her "dancing," he refers to it as "this dancing business") belated, while at the same time, and this makes him even more against it, he knows she gave it up way back when. Of her own free will, of course—that is important to him, the fact that it was her own decision, shortly after they got married—he didn't push her to do it, she just fell victim to circumstance: the long trip into the city, then pregnancy, then the house, which didn't clean itself. A phrase that came from her and not from him, and which she applied in some form to everything imaginable: the meal, which wouldn't cook itself. The children, who wouldn't raise themselves.

And now she wants to start hopping around again? Or in her words, dancing? Now? While her body might remember, it's also gotten a little wider around the hips, so much so that when she's doing little demonstrations for him, he makes an effort not to look there but at her ankles, which have remained quite slender. Does she really want to know how he sees it? That her teacher is nothing to him? Just average and mediocre? And another note: he should consider himself lucky to have landed here in their beautiful suburb, and there would probably be just as much flourishing going on here as in a gym somewhere else—and where would that be anyway?

But alas, he says: "Yes. It's too bad for him. But if he is as good as you say—"

"'Good' is an understatement."

"Well, if he is incredible, then it's a win for all of you!"

She hadn't looked at it that way. But yes, she says: "Yes, you're right!"

Some peace. If it weren't all so exhausting. Sometimes he thinks he really does have something wrong with his heart. Some flap that closes when it is supposed to open that's putting his life in mortal danger without his having the slightest clue. An idea that sets his heart racing. Anyway, he's not sweating anymore. Even with being out and about so much. Strange. When he and Jordan were playing catch, he didn't break a sweat once. What might he be up to? At this very moment? Perhaps he's drawing a picture of him to give it to his mother: *A day with Grandpa* scrawled underneath to make her happy. And she hangs it up somewhere she'll be able to see it as soon as she gets home from work, because it cheers her up.

That petal, has it fallen yet? He thinks he can hear it fall while his wife practices the moves she's relearning. The edge of the dining table serves as a barre. "A little too low," but she needs something to hold on to. And she dances over the precipice with both feet, suddenly lets go—he feels dizzy.

"Here, quick. Have some water!" Is he able to see?

He nods.

She holds the glass up to his lips, but it's tilted too high, and the water runs down his chin; he pushes it away so forcefully the rest spills onto the floor. A puddle with lamplight inside, a few drops that escaped. He hears an alert on the TV: Time for the evening news? What could that be? That faint ringing? Ah, the phone. It rings three times.

"Probably just a telemarketer," says his wife. "They usually call in the evening."

She is standing over the puddle as if she's been planted there, empty glass in hand. He passed out shortly after she did the pirouette, and she still had the one leg bent, she shows him, when all of a sudden he turned white and tipped backward, like in slow motion.

"A little dizzy spell," he says, and his voice sounds strange, like it's coming from far away, as if he weren't sitting here but over there, not inside the house but outside the door, on the moss-covered steps, and he shakes his head as if to unplug his ears, as if they were filled with water after a dip in the puddle, which is vanishing now because his wife is wiping it up with a rag that isn't all that absorbent.

"A giveaway," she explains. "They just called to ask if we wanted more of it."

But he can't make sense of her words. What is she talking about? And where on earth is Jordan? He should have come home as soon as it got dark, like they agreed on.

"Jordan who?"

"Oh, our grandson." Isn't she worried about him at all? "He is so small," he says, and only when his wife is staring at him, clearly confused, does he realize he is playing a game whose rules she doesn't know. "A little dizzy spell," he repeats, and his voice sounds closer now, as if he were sitting next to himself.

Little by little, the daze that's come over him wears off, and he even manages to get upset that the man on TV—the presenter, that's what he's called—apparently has a speech impediment. Every word seems to be drawn out, or is that from his ears too? He feels like he's been sucked into the screen. Sees himself sitting in the circle with the others.

"Mr Katō," someone asks him, "what does the word *no* mean to you?" And he stares into the camera. Stammers: "Well, I don't . . . *know*." Everyone laughs.

Now his wife is massaging his neck. "So many knots," she says. The smell of camphor drifts down from his shoulders. "It's a good thing you just bought this ointment."

Didn't buy it, got it as a gift. From Mr Medicine Man. But he is too weak to tell her the whole story. He'd have to go all the way back to the cemetery for her to understand. And really even further than that, to the teenagers on the plastic bench, the seafood curry, the poems from years ago, and night will have fallen in the meantime, a long, very long night, and by the time morning comes, he still wouldn't be through.

"Not so hard!" he hollers. "That hurts!"

So instead, she runs her fingers gently up and down his spine. Asks him if he is still thinking of getting him? The white Pomeranian? She has given it some thought.

With his last bit of strength, he manages to say: "You can't be serious. It's out of the question! It's just a childish fantasy."

A husband who doesn't say a word. And no backstory this time. The woman—on the tape Mie describes her as a woman of sixty, Chieko—already has a husband she texts regularly, which is why she struggles to find words to say out loud and has already developed numerous clearly psychological grievances: a lump in her throat that seems permanent now along with an itchy rash around her mouth, a slight stutter, which always flares up when someone calls her by her last name, though not by her first name.

She hasn't been called "Chieko" for an eternity, and never by her husband, who says it makes no sense, she knows what her name is. She hadn't wanted to send a photo, the reason being there weren't any she liked herself in. And it seemed an inconvenience to supply one that she doesn't even recognize herself in anymore, which is the case with the ones where she's younger. There's no point in sending them.

"Sheesh. It's a lot, isn't it? She is desperate to talk. But that makes it easier on you—your only job is to keep your mouth shut. Use her first name every now and again, but only when it seems right, that would make her very happy." Otherwise: "Just laze the day away! You will meet by the entrance to the aquarium, that's the spot she chose. Deep-sea creatures are her favorite animals. And, oh yes, this is how you'll know her: she'll be wearing a yolk-colored dress that she is having altered for the occasion, though tighter or looser she didn't say, but I'll bet looser. She was twenty the last time she wore it.

"In the event that another woman is standing at the meeting spot wearing a yolk-colored dress, which is quite possible, as I tried to explain to her but not very likely, you'll be able to tell because she's accessorizing with a red umbrella. If it ends up raining, which is much more likely, it'll be opened. These details seemed important to her: Yolk-colored and red. Tucked in and opened. But I can assure you: apart from all this whimsy, she's very down-to-earth and didn't give the impression on the phone that she had anything else in mind other than just look- ing at fish, and in the process, getting some things off her chest. As for your name?" she adds a little mischievously. "She says that's neither here nor there."

CHAPTER TWENTY

Expecting a jellyfish, he is surprised when he sees her standing in the distance (it is in fact raining) under her opened umbrella: a slip of a woman, thinner than thin, as if someone had drawn her on a sheet of paper with a pencil and then gone over her with an eraser. Almost fully erased. And had there been no yolk-colored dress and red umbrella, he would have looked straight through her, only been able to ascertain by the second glance that, no, this was not a mirage. There is a person waiting there.

He starts toward her, zigzagging to avoid the puddles. When he finally reaches her, he feels like he has covered a great distance.

"There you are." She smiles at him.

Her skin is pulled taut, he can make out her skull underneath, her upper and lower jaw, nasal ridge, and cheekbones. But her rash—red blisters which are partially dried up, but partially as fresh as if they'd just formed—give this skeletal woman a certain vivacity, and he is hit with the thought that she needs it, the rash, to remind herself and him of the flesh still encasing her. He can't bring himself to utter a *hello,* the one word he had wanted to say despite his instructions, so instead, he nods, mute as the fish waving visitors toward the entrance with its fin, and as he bobs his head up and down, he thinks he can feel the vertebrae in his neck, each individual one, feels the way they're stacked on top of each other, discs between them.

"Let's dive in." She smiles, and this time, she shows her teeth.

White teeth. Smooth and stainless. Dentures, he thinks. What if they fall out? Terrifying. But she has looped her arm in his, and he once again has the distinct sensation he can feel his bones under the almost-undetectable weight of her arm, and although he is the stronger one, she is the one doing the pulling, directing him around and carting him along behind her.

"This," she says, "is where I feel happy," and points to the glass ceiling above their heads where a ray is gliding by.

The cash register is shaped like a dolphin; a cashier stands in its mouth and exchanges entry tickets for cash. He feels like someone who is invited onto a roller coaster even though he doesn't want to go on the ride, the difference being in that situation he could stand his ground—he can't do that here, in the depths of the ocean. Luckily, he doesn't have to say anything. A soft crunch. He is gritting his teeth.

"Pretty, isn't it?" First the freshwater fish. They stroll from room to room and stop in front of the crawfish for a while. "If you look closely, you can see the marbling on the shell. You can't see that? Look, just there! You have to come closer to the glass!"

She talks as if he were talking back to her, she asks questions, explains, answers follow-up questions. "You know what? We used to come here quite a bit. Well, by 'used to,' I mean when we first got together. All right: back then. Not that often,

you say? Well, maybe a dozen times. I call that often. You don't?
So you don't agree. In that case: just a few times. But it was nice,
wasn't it? You have to agree with me there, at least? That it was
nice?"

And although he isn't saying anything, only listening to
her in silence, as he was told, he feels increasingly cast into the
role of someone who is taking every word she says and twisting
it until she runs out of things to say, except for the extremely
vague *nice*. He would be happy to let her have it, this *nice,* but
the other word swooped in to replace it, transforming it into an
even vaguer *lovely. Lovely* could perhaps be used for a natural
event, like the northern lights or a group of shooting stars. Not
a trip to the aquarium, where nature is essentially just pretense.
She should, before she opens her mouth, think about what it is
exactly that she means to say; otherwise, what comes out ends
up being just a lot of nonsense.

"But—" She searches in vain for a defense. In the end, *lovely*
stays. She unloops her arm from his and grabs at her throat with
her erased hand, but she can't get rid of the lump that's formed
there, even without her adversary being there, only in her mind.

By the time they get to the ocean creatures, she's a little more
tired. And maybe because he called her Chieko once, which
made her turn as red as a schoolgirl, and with her rash now a bit
faded, she begins, breathing easier with every pool they pass, to
tell the starfish, seahorses, and sea urchins about him and the
suffering he causes her, which he doesn't want to believe. She
asks them to excuse his name, calling it ugly and an attack on
him; she would understand if he doesn't want to hear it aloud.

"RHS—retired husband syndrome," she says tersely, staring into space, which makes him think of his real wife with a longing he hasn't felt for her in a long time. Maybe they should come here too, laze a day away. When he left the house this morning, she asked what he had planned, but before he could even respond with some negligible answer, she went into the garden; the pine tree, she murmured as she walked away, needed trimming.

I could fly to the moon, he thought, *and it wouldn't change a thing,* which he then called after her as a joke: "In that case, I'm going to the moon!" But of course she did not hear him. And if she had, what could she have said to that? *Safe travels*? *Have fun*? *Come back soon*? Well. At least that would be something to do, he thinks now and even more wistfully than before: go on a trip, not necessarily here, but maybe, why not, to the ocean? Sit on a straw mat and eat rice balls and hard-boiled eggs, all while trying not to get any sand between your teeth. An uncomfortable sensation. The fantasy brings him back to Chieko.

"RHS," she repeats, suddenly looking straight into his eyes. "I know your thoughts on illness. The way you see it, only people with no backbone get sick. And while that might be true"— she shrugs—"not everyone is a shark like you, there are so many different ways of being in the world. I am someone who will get eaten, while you are someone who does the eating, and that's why I have to be careful around you. You could say it's a rule of nature. And along those same lines. You don't hurt me. You're just there. And oh, you're there, all right. You're there from morning 'til night! And I don't know how to say this to make you understand, but your being there necessitates my not-being there. Simple as that.

"Take last night, when you were telling me how to hold my chopsticks; I was holding them like a child just learning how to eat, and I was trying to hold them properly, just like you showed me, but then I started trembling; it was imperceptible at first, was it not? You didn't notice. And then all at once I no longer knew how to do it at all, hold chopsticks. It was like I had never held them before. So you showed me again; you were very patient with me. But the shock of it. That stayed—and will stay—with me for a long, long time.

"You didn't intend for that. I know. You're worried about me? The more I threaten to slip away from you, the more you want to be there? To be there any less is physically impossible. You are there! there! there! Some days just hearing you swallow, hearing the sound your tongue makes, is enough to set my whole body shaking, and even though you don't say anything, not a single word, it's as if you want to tell me how to breathe, which makes it so that I can't take another breath. I am sorry. I know you mean to do well by me." And with a glance at the moray eel lurking between the rocks: "Terribly well."

"They changed the upholstery. It used to be beige."

When they find a spot to sit in the canteen—designed like the belly of a humpback whale, with its swelling and contracting song playing over the loudspeakers—she orders five chocolate cupcakes. The waitress asks timidly whether she should pack some up for them, she has to-go boxes, 10 percent recyclable.

"No." Chieko laughs. "They're for here. And a coffee for my husband. He takes it with just a splash of milk. Not too much.

Just a dash should do it, about this much." She indicates the amount with her fingers. And turning to him as the waitress is typing in their order: "Too much milk will make you constipated."

His mouth goes dry. He swallows. How had it happened, he wonders, between the high and low notes of the whale, that she, the woman, suddenly turned into the man, and he, the man, suddenly became the woman. The roles reversed. And the fact that something like this happens, he thinks. It snuck in somehow, became a habit, and that's the way it's been ever since. Each person trapped in their role, waiting to be released, which will never happen.

"Marriage," says Chieko, "is like being in the belly of a whale. You sit in darkness knowing the other person is just a few meters away. You call out to them, they call back. But no matter how you do it, whether you just sit there listening or set off on your own way, feeling your way blindly through the bowels, you can't find one another, and the only thing you have in common is the darkness. And with that"—she waits for the waitress to turn off her tablet—"it's over. I am divorcing you."

A moment of surprise.

The waitress looks first at her, then at him, and finally reverts to the lines she is required to say: "We are honored to be able to serve you. Please enjoy."

"Thank you very much." Chieko turns over her plate and removes the plastic film from the cupcakes. She pops her fingers into her mouth one by one to lick off the chocolate still clinging to them. "Mmm, delicious!" she says, delighted. "Even better than before! Pardon me: back then!" But the word choice is no longer important. She has pulled a photo out of her purse. "Do you remember this? I'm wearing the same yolk-colored dress; it's shortly before we got married. You called me your little dumpling." A woman, fatter than fat, as if someone had thrown a bucket of paint at the wall and then kept going over it again and again.

"Granted, my arms were a little large, but see how happy I look. What, you don't see it? Look closer." And she brings it up to his nose, he inhales it, her former happiness. "You were the skinnier one. Now it's the other way around. And if we'd stayed like that, maybe—but we didn't. Now, there are certain things, you have to agree, that can't be undone, which is why I'm here: the form."

She sets a sheet of paper in front of him, along with a Sharpie—*Why no pen?* he thinks helplessly—she had even brought his seal along.

"I beg you to just let it be. Do you see? I'm not upset with you. That's not what this is about. If you just, down there, where the box is. And no, you don't have to say anything now, don't try to talk me out of it. Just sign." She covers her ears. "You have to sign it! It'll only take a second. Don't you know how to hold it? The marker? You have to hold it at an angle—like this—a little more slanted! We can sort out the rest later. I don't want anything from you. Not the house or your money. And please, don't worry about me. I have some money set aside. It will be enough to make ends meet for now."

"But, Chieko!" he whispers.

But she has begun to eat, devouring one cupcake after the

other. When she's done, she orders five strawberry charlottes. "What, you don't carry them anymore? Then the Mont Blancs! Yes, five!" Not to go, but to eat here.

He sighs.

CHAPTER TWENTY-ONE

Rule number four: We don't take it personally. It doesn't matter what it is, it could be a profession of love or a divorce, but we never lose sight of the fact that we are a tool, not a person with their own wants and desires, because our wanting—isn't this the case?—only leads to more wanting. I couldn't care less about what you do in your own life; take things personally all you want! But not when you're working as a stand-in. You have to be strict about this. Sorry."

"But"—he shudders—"I had to take it personally. I mean, it was bad enough not to be able to say anything, especially when it came to the constipation comment, but the way she jumped for joy before the seal had even dried and wagged the piece of paper through the air, it was worse than anything that has ever happened to me. And oh, how she cheered! It was shameless! I felt ashamed for her to my core; someone had to be. And with the whale sounds playing the whole time in the background, just awful. It sounded like someone was dying. And you're saying that shouldn't be taken personally? Dying?"

"You're really getting into it now!" Mie laughs. She's finally laughing again. "Take it down a notch!" Today, she is Sayuri, a daughter who has been dead for fifteen years, whose parents, still grieving, want to sit next to her one more time. See how much she's grown. Hear what her voice sounds like. Feel how her hand, once that of a young girl, has turned into a young woman's. A job she normally wouldn't take. "You never play anyone dead." But the parents had cried so much. The father even more than the mother, although he hadn't shed a single tear, and she went through an entire box of tissues. "An unequal distribution here too, but that doesn't seem to be that big of an issue in marriages."

"No, not at all! Take me and my wife, for instance," and he has an urge to tell her about the front steps and that it is actually his responsibility to remove the moss, but his wife had been kind enough to take it on because of his heart condition, although, he keeps this part to himself, it isn't true. No matter which way you look at it: nothing about it is true. "We complete each other," he says. "But it could be that we're the exception. No matter! Back to Chieko. What I felt ashamed about, more than her cheering, is this: that her rash, as soon as we left the belly of the whale, just disappeared, as if by magic. Not a trace. And she was beaming! It wasn't even a real divorce, just a fake one, and the piece of paper I signed was just a blank sheet with a little box she had drawn herself. Nothing legal about it. A farce. And yet she was beaming with the light of a thousand suns—when we parted she was beside herself with joy."

"Typical RHS." Mie had seen a few cases. "A kind of un-diseasing, if there is such a thing. Or to put it differently: a healthy way of standing up for yourself." He can look up exactly what that means at home. "You're the kind of guy who likes to look things up, aren't you?"

"Who, me?"

"Yes, you. Or is there someone else I'm speaking to?" She looks over his shoulder. "As it happens, there is someone! Not bad"—a quiet whistle—"you played guitar when you were younger, didn't you? Or no, give me a second—you were a poet! That seems more accurate. I see the unkempt hair, the long nights spent filling up page after page, which your wife found attractive and still does to this day. A man with feelings, an exception, you could say!"

"Oh, stop it! What would you know?"

"A lot," she says. "But more on that another time, I have to be on my way again soon. It wouldn't be right for a dead person to be late. Rule number five: We pay attention to punctuality and don't let our loved ones wait for us for more than a minute. One minute goes by quickly. Two minutes, in comparison, seems like half a lifetime. Which brings us to your next assignment: A Mr Terazawa Hiroshi asked you to speak at his wedding. You are his boss. But don't worry, you won't be alone. I'm a sister again, an older sister this time, and I'll be able to keep an eye on you from a distance."

"And the colleagues? I mean—"

"—all stand-ins," she cuts him off. "This is a major under-taking, and we have teamed up with a partner agency for the occasion. The only real people are the bride and groom. And you should have seen them when they came into my office yes-terday. You're only that young and in love once in your life. Here's the speech. I prepared it for you, along with photos and a list of everyone in attendance. In addition, the tape, as usual; you should know how this goes by now.

"By the way, you should still be working on your smile. Keep up the good work! You have improved quite a bit, but you have to keep at it. What if you painted red dots on your toes? Little things like that often turn out to make a big difference."

And with that, she gets up. She is wearing a pantsuit and holding a briefcase. Sayuri has obviously become a career woman.

CHAPTER TWENTY-TWO

He forgot to greet the mice. But by the time he remembers, he is already almost at his front door. Should he go back again? But then he sees his wife waving at him from the window. A glitch in time. The last time she did this was when the children were small. Returning from work, he always knew: just one more turn! Then he would be able to see her waving. And he'd hurry to get past the last curve, leaning forward a little more, pressing his feet a little harder off the ground, until finally he saw her, so *petite* standing there in her white apron, she almost took his breath away: how lucky he was! A woman like that in a house like this with children like theirs, if only they would stay this small forever!

But at some point, he started staying in town until late at night, he had been promised a promotion and had to prove he was a team player. In addition, the loan wouldn't pay off itself. An expression that came from him, not from her, and he applied it to almost everything: The gas and electric and phone bills. The housekeeping allowance. At first his wife waited up to serve him his dinner, but as it gradually got later and later, he would come home to find the house mostly dark, with only one solitary light left on in the entryway.

The dinner would be cold, left out for him on the table, but he was too exhausted to even take one bite. And at some point, she stopped putting it out at all. In any case, he ate out. So she could save herself the trouble. A word that filled him with satisfaction: *save*. Apparently, she had adapted. There was always a can of beer in the fridge, that remained, and the hiss when he opened it didn't disturb the silence that surrounded him; on the contrary, it seemed to make the silence a little bit quieter. *They're asleep,* he thought, and felt like a man returning home from war, letting his loved ones sleep while he rummaged around in the kitchen, still awake.

He knew where his wife hid the cigarettes. In the cupboard behind the mason jars. She had taken to having one as soon as the children were in bed, and once he caught her smoking one cold winter night, outside on the patio, and she didn't put it out straightaway, instead came puffing out of the shadow of the pine tree.

"What's this? You're back already?" she asked.

And it pained him to see how little she resembled the woman who had once waved at him, so that now he had to search for her, the resemblance, found it finally in the way she added mischievously: "Nice to see you again! Would you like one too?" She held out the pack. And they smoked like teenagers, one last one, and then another last one, standing there shivering, side by side, blowing smoke into the air.

"It smells like snow," he said.

And as if he had summoned it, in that moment, it began to snow. Small white flakes that landed on their heads as they huddled a little closer together, so close they grew warm and, despite the cold, preferred to stay outside, didn't want to go back in.

"Just think! We're going to be grandparents!"

His wife met him with a wide smile. Since when does she wear lipstick? And what on earth had she done to her hair? A perm. She did it because, well. There was no real reason. She was just in the mood for a change. And she told him about their daughter, who called earlier to say that the insemination—the fourth, mind you—had finally been successful.

"What? The insemination?" This was the first time he was hearing about this. Or had she mentioned it last night at dinner, but he had begged her to talk about something more appetizing?

"Oh, we've been through all this, she's been having a tough go of it. But now"—sighing, relieved—"all is well!" She made it past the twelfth week of pregnancy. "And from the looks of it, she was at the ultrasound today, it's ninety percent a boy!"

"Only ninety?" He tries to picture a 90 percent boy.

"That's as accurate as they could get."

The baby had turned sideways, and they couldn't get close enough from underneath. But the main thing is, hands and feet! Everything was there! He shouldn't worry about the remaining 10 percent, which makes him grumble to himself, and she gives him a pinch as if to wake him up, calls him *Grandpa*, laughing, and then sets the slippers in front of him so he'll be able to slide right into them. A gesture, he thinks, that is almost like a hug, and he feels hugged by her.

Now would be the moment to say something. But what?

Something that fits the occasion. That he is delighted, that it's high time their daughter got pregnant, why did they even wait this long? Or that they should drive out to visit her, if only she weren't so far away, all the way on the other side of the country, and in such a cramped area. Not a single decent hotel around. Maybe it would be better if she came to them, she hasn't been home in ages. He doesn't like to think about the last time they stayed there.

She put them on the couch in her living room, and for an entire night, he had lain next to his wife unable to sleep, because he didn't know how to do it anymore: be next to her. Apparently, he had gotten used to having his own bed after all. He only grasps the loss in hindsight. And his back pain! He would have preferred to sleep on the floor, which in fact is exactly what he did the next night, covered in nothing but a thin sheet, and then woken up with a bad cold. The son-in-law joked that his father was the exact same.

"What do you mean, *same*?" he wanted to know.

"Oh, just a little old-fashioned."

He just didn't get that it was more comfortable on the floor than the couch, which was apparently a generational difference, and after this they left earlier than planned, early afternoon instead of late afternoon. He had brooded over the whole thing the entire train ride back. He wasn't old-fashioned, he was—he couldn't think of the word—"difficult," said his wife. And she said this as if to herself but still loud enough for him to hear it, but he was too tired to ask her what she meant; he hadn't gotten a wink of sleep for two nights in a row now, and his nose was so stuffed up he couldn't get any air through.

In spite of this, he forced himself to watch the landscape passing by the window, to appear as interested as he could, though he didn't make out anything, really. Leafed noisily through a book without reading. Pretended to be asleep and wished to himself that she would rouse him awake. Just this once. Keep him from retreating.

"RHS," he reads. The letters flicker on the screen, and he squints to see them better. An abbreviation for this so-called *retired husband syndrome,* a psychosomatic condition, the cause of which is to be found in increasing estrangement between husband and wife, which in a traditional marriage is deemed insurmountable in many cases around the time of the husband's retirement. Symptoms include stress, insomnia, speech disorders, and skin irritations among other things, because the traditional housewife is unable to get used to the constant presence of her husband, experiencing it instead as an anxiety-inducing strain. His presence seems to cling to her like a wet towel, hence the expression "Wet towel," which allegorically—

—he clicks out of the page.

"What nonsense," he snorts. They need to pull themselves together. And he isn't sure exactly who he means by that. The husbands or the wives. "Inventing problems where there are none to begin with! And the doctors make a killing. How two people get on is a private matter, but in today's world, you have to drag everything out in the open and label it with the most inflammatory names possible. That makes it sell better, a trick of the pharma industry, and we fall for it and pop their pills instead of . . . It's a giant bubble!"

And he clicks back again so that he can go on ranting about it some more. The retired breadwinner is a proverbial load of garbage lying around the house, in the way and not good for anything, which is why it is all the more important that he gives some thought beforehand to how he plans to spend his retirement. Unfortunately, it is all too often the case that outside of his professional life he's failed to either acquire a circle of friends or pick up any meaningful activities, an error that will come back to haunt him later.

And with that, a link to professional help. There are psychiatric clinics scattered around where you can sign up as someone affected. One of them, he snorts again, is quite close by, not that far from his doctor. Reviews and advice forums, a whole flood of posts from anonymous sufferers. And he wonders why people need this, to unburden themselves under the cloak of anonymity. To show off? Or perhaps to hide better? Maybe both, he thinks, and scrolls back to the top. Reads the word *estrangement* again and that in many cases it proves an "insurmountable obstacle."

"Utter nonsense," he says again, but this time more quietly and without making a fuss. After that, he types in the name of the fitness studio, Fit for Life, and among the dance courses looks for the one for fifty-plus. He has studied the instructor's photo numerous times before, and as soon as it's looming there in front of him, he is surprised by how little he feels when he's confronted by the bulge in the man's tight pants, and alternately by how much he feels reading his bio, which he now almost knows by heart: Studied in Moscow and Paris. Years of dancing on stages across the globe. Then an injury. Rehab. Finally, the return home, where he reinvented himself. A fairy tale, he thinks, but without the usual grimness. He has to force himself to think that at all.

Then he shuts down the computer and sits motionless for a while in front of the black screen. He could unpack his suitcase. Lift the woodpecker on his desk. Spend the rest of the day watching him peck at the tree trunk. But no. That would be too sad. Better organize his records then. Not alphabetically, he got that far in the decision-making process at least, he has another idea now: sorted according to the point in his life when he first listened to it? So he pulls the first record tentatively off the shelf, but immediately pushes it back in again; the time when his wife made a pilgrimage through the city to hunt it down seems too far away, she did it after he had only mentioned once, in a casual aside—they hadn't been married yet—that it happened to be one of his favorite records. And this makes him think that the only time he listened to music was back in the day.

In recent years, he has never once listened with the same devotion, or with the sense that his hands and feet are listening too, which is why—he runs his fingers over it—the collection can remain just as it is, in the very disarray it is in now. Trying to create order here would be like trying to run forward while running backward. With every step forward, he would be distancing himself from his goal. Better to stay put. He blows the dust off his fingers. So. One more thing to check off his list.

CHAPTER TWENTY-THREE

When he asks his wife to please iron the white shirt he last wore over eight years ago, at their daughter's wedding, she doesn't ask any questions, which on the one hand he is happy about, because it saves him from having to come up with another lie, but on the other disappoints him, because of how much faith she has in him. She could have at least asked whether the shirt still fits him, because he has put on a bit of weight after all, and it would have been nice if she had pointed it out to him, because then he could have replied that it was because of all the delicious food she had been making lately, that he noticed all the effort she was putting in. But she missed her chance, and, mind you, she's the one missing out, not he. It's just a shame she doesn't know.

Her indifference sitting there at the ironing board, humming a melody that seems to absorb her whole being, is worse than the lie he would have had to invent, and he grows suspicious, starts circling her, getting closer and closer. That wrinkle there, on the left shoulder, might she have missed it? No, the shoulders come after the button strip. If he could just be patient! Steam rises from the iron and she continues her humming.

"That's a pretty tune," he says.

"You think so?"

"Very pretty."

Where is it from? From the dance studio. Of course. The instructor plays it over and over again when they're practicing their arabesques—in any case, a term that comes from the ornamental, does he know what it means? And now she can't get it out of her head, she's stretched back her leg to it so often. It was torture. "But"—she pulls the fabric taut—"it's nice to have someone who pushes you to your limit, then you know what you're really capable of. And what you're not." Anyhow, she needs to work on her lower back, it's atrophied over the years, and she hadn't known which muscles were still even there. And now she knows.

"Because it's sore! It's sad if you think about it, don't you think? That something has to hurt for you to know it's there?"

Her instructor teacher put it this way: "Without pain, there is no memory, and without memory, the body would not be dancing." And the urgency in his words made them all very anxious.

"Of course, by *dancing,* he meant *life.* Clever, don't you think?"

He finds it flat and unoriginal, but doesn't say so. A windbag! And he sits down because he's feeling dizzy again. Not now! Please, not now! He tries to focus on a single point, but on which one, he wonders, there are so many. The back of his wife's neck as she continues to iron, the rising steam that immediately dissipates again, the shirtsleeve resting on her knees, her lower back, full of forgotten muscles. All points that could connect to form a perfect geometric figure. He closes his eyes but only for a moment, then he opens them again. The dizziness has let up. Had he been at the doctor's? Found out more about his heart?

"Yes," he said. "Business as usual. Nothing to worry about. A little irregularity, probably stress-related." He bites his tongue. If she would ask anything further, he would explain to her that being retired doesn't make you immune to stress; nowadays, you're at risk even in old age. There are studies proving this, from reputable researchers devoted solely to this subject but whose names he can't seem to remember right now. But she doesn't ask any more about it.

"Mm-hmm," is all she says. Hangs his shirt on a hanger on the door. Checks the collar one more time. "Satisfied?"

He nods.

She exhales.

CHAPTER TWENTY-FOUR

You were shocked, I could tell. That someone would want to get married without any of their relatives, or just run off and get married in Vegas if that's the case, just the two of them, and they end up renting a whole company instead. But people have their reasons, and they're always different. For the Terazawas, it's a matter of perfection. They actually had the celebration already, and from what they told me, it sounds like a total disaster. A drunk father, hysterical mother, aunt and uncle who topped it all off with a brawl involving even you, the boss, as well as a handful of friends, and don't ask me how or where it came from, but a circus monkey who couldn't help but—I won't say it—but—on the guests' heads!—such an unpleasant situation that nobody will look back on it fondly, least of all the bride and groom, who have since—

"Oh, but what am I even saying? You'll have to forgive me! Here I try to save us both some time but start telling non-truths. And why? To warm up. Because the truth is much different, it always is, and much more depressing at that, and I can hardly bring myself to share it with you. Hence the monkey. Isn't that right? A little joke? And you understand I would have preferred the version where he you-know-whats on their heads? But he didn't. There was no celebration. And as far as the relatives, there will never be any, because the bride, a Ms Furui Sakura, doesn't have much longer to live, with any luck maybe another six months. A situation which doesn't, let's face it, have the best outlook; both of them understand that their marriage is a kind of early funeral, with the advantage being that the bride is still alive and the whole thing won't be a tragic grief-fest but instead a celebration.

"Please smile now! Or if you can't, then try a little grin at least. I'm trying my best to keep things lighthearted. Because that's what Sakura wants: to be allowed to slip out of her pajamas and into a wedding dress for a few hours, not more than an afternoon, to take off her breathing mask and say, 'I do,' and kiss the groom on the lips. And if no one approves, then at least we do, the pretend ones. By the way, they didn't actually come to my office. I lied because I was embarrassed. I didn't want you to have to confront death right away; after all, this is only your third assignment. I visited her in the hospital. Everything else is true: they are young and in love! And *[Mie smiles; he can hear her smiling]* unbelievably attractive! An attractiveness that seems to cling to them both despite all the ugliness—the narrow hospital bed and the spit bowl, the IV and the tubes—an attractiveness you wish would last forever, but only because there is a time limit.

"But that isn't even true, it's cruel is what it is. A truth you tape together and then leave there like it's part of the furniture. If Sakura hadn't thrown up multiple times, I would have thought she was fine. A little banged-up after a long night, but nothing an aspirin couldn't fix. I would have thought she could get up at any time, get dressed, go outside for a walk. It's unbelievable how little of death you can see in her. Only life! And more life! She keeps a record of all the little things that bring her joy; she showed it to me. She wrote something down on each page. The sound of rain against the window. Pureed pancakes for lunch. Hiroshi teaching her to whistle. Light falling in stripes across her feet. An honest word. The doctor with the goatee she wants to touch. A whole list of little things that together make up her life, and I was surprised when she said that none of them belonged to her; she said it was enough just to be able to hold on to them for a moment.

"That's how their wedding should be too, there should be nothing concrete about it. No vows in the traditional sense, really just a party so she can sip some champagne again, because she so seldom got the opportunity to do so. Her parents, Hiroshi added, didn't think it was right, you don't drink champagne in the face of death, but they both wanted this one last act of resistance—they said parents' rules are for people who have a lot of time left.

"The two of them have thought through everything; they planned it down to the last detail! We, the professionals, barely have anything left to do. I know, I even joked they should become wedding planners and help me out with future projects, which gave them both a good laugh. Something small that might end up back in Sakura's book: a joke that isn't funny, but still made them laugh anyway. Please forgive me."

[A rustling, then silence—he wonders if the tape is broken— after a moment Mie's voice comes back on, husky.]

"The photos, do you have them in front of you? The one with them on the Ferris wheel. Do you see how blue the sky is? The

only marks are from an airplane, and it looks like they're float-
ing, while the houses and cars, and the crowd of people stuck on
the ground. This photo hits her the hardest. She is so high up,
while down below everything is so infinitely small. Keep that
in the back of your mind during your speech. How much space
there is up there. We owe it to them both to get to there. I'm
afraid if we don't, we won't reach them."

    *[No word of goodbye. No "Stop." The tape continues to play,
without Mie saying anything more.]*

CHAPTER TWENTY-FIVE

When they meet in front of the wedding chapel, he feels like he's on a film set, everything is buzzing with excitement, though he stays mindful of the task at hand. Last-minute instructions, then gifts and money envelopes are passed out, then comes the groom, his mother adjusting his pocket square. And she's sniffling, she makes you want to reach out and give her shoulder a little squeeze, say: "It's all right!" His father greets all the relatives, some of whom have traveled a long way, and asks if they'd like anything to drink.

The way it comes out makes it sound like an order. Clearly a beginner. Or could he be talking like that on purpose? Because fathers are usually gruff? Snacks and drinks are passed around. He, the boss, helps himself to as much as he likes and strikes up conversations with his colleagues, who haven't forgotten that he is the boss and are each trying to outdo the other in their courtesy toward him. And he enjoys their display of submissiveness and automatically adopts the posture of their superior, speaks loudly while they speak softly, walks ahead of them up the steps to the chapel, is the first to take his seat while they, meanwhile, are still standing. A hierarchy that is familiar to him.

When he was still working, he often practiced in front of the mirror how to give the person opposite him a specific kind of look, one full of authority, but in the end, he was always disillusioned when he realized he was the one standing there looking at himself this way, and that he, with his eyes so suddenly sunken in, would never get much further than where he already was. But all that helps him now. He knows how they feel standing next to him. They straighten up when he leans back, and he knows they're feeling hot, and he isn't.

Mie, the older sister, is handing out little bags of flower petals for afterward, when the couple leaves to go outside. He gives her a nod, she nods back. The bridesmaids scurry past, giggling.

"It's about to start!" someone calls.

And: "She's here!"

The sound of a car door opening and closing. Every head is turned toward the entrance.

"The bride!"

And she walks in, bathed in light that follows her from outside, and everyone is craning for a glimpse; there she is striding down the aisle on her father's arm, draped in ruffles and lace, an abundance of fabric, so much it is impossible to recognize her underneath. But then she lifts her veil, and a murmur ripples through the crowd. The organ plays one final bar. The colleague to his left falls out of character for a moment.

"She looks even better than the photos," he whispers, nudging him in his side.

And even the pastor, a foreign student, is at a loss for words, clears his throat several times, apparently without success, before he finally raises his voice, but even then it just comes out in a stammer. And he wonders if he is pretending—if the emotion with which he preaches about marriage and its being a lasting promise, a constant give-and-take that those committed will practice for all eternity—whether this emotion is real or just for show, the sweat on his brow fake or real, whether his glance down at the page, like he's lost his train of thought, is feigned or desperate, because the text simply doesn't measure up to the beauty of this dying woman.

And he wonders, too, whether they aren't all dying in that sense, without really understanding it, or wanting to understand, except in moments like these, that they are in the process of dying all the time? The blind grandfather, truly blind, according to Mie, although—she wasn't sure—he seems to be able to see a little bit, is staring spellbound at the bride, his granddaughter, he can still remember her as a little girl, how warm and soft her little cheeks used to feel. He looks at the couple before him—the groom had just been on his smartphone, so his girlfriend had stepped on his toe, now he's pocketed it and she moves close, so that their bodies become one, no space between them.

The fat aunt, the plane ride almost did her in, it was so cramped, but she was telling everyone that the trip cost a third less because her nephew, the groom, booked it for her well in advance, that's the kind of person he is. Everyone understands, no matter whether they're acting or not, that in this moment they are just as beautiful as what they're witnessing, even if they won't want to understand it a minute from now, instead scattering away from each other again, back to their houses, where maybe they will happen upon a petal later that got caught in their collar. Which will bring them back for a moment. And then they'll fall asleep.

His speech. Nothing special. A eulogy for one of his most capable employees, whom he knows is now in good hands, though he hopes this won't affect his motivation but increase it. And yet. Reciting sentence after sentence as the couple looks on, holding hands, already a little tired—her especially, she had hardly been able to make it to the ballroom and had to be carried the last few meters by him, because she, according to the whispers going around, does not want to use her wheelchair today—he begins to feel something he had been waiting to feel at his own daughter's wedding but that never arrived, despite some effort on his part to pull it out of himself: what it really feels like to give up your own child, to pass them off to someone else without wanting to hold on to even a little piece of them. And he feels his shirt tightening around his chest, the collar closing in around his neck, his buttons and cuffs pulling him down with a weight that collects in his middle and then rises, slowly, as a tear slips from his smiling eye.

"Dearest Sakura," he says, "this is about turning someone into a man. And for that, I thank you in the name of our company, whom from now on you can call family."

It's not a hollow phrase. He means it. And the applause that comes as he is navigating his way down from the podium back to his spot, is not hollow applause, either. They keep clapping long after he is sitting down. The program is next, first the wedding dance, and then photos are projected onto a screen from a not-so-distant childhood. Hiroshi in a kiddie pool. Sakura with a water gun. The photos resemble one another, almost interchangeable—he believes he can see his own son and daughter in them, he sees them lying there in the light of the moon, how big they've gotten, and he resolves to do something with them very soon, a walk in the woods perhaps, and he will show them how to tell which way is north and which way is south, you can read it from the moss, but how did this happen?

They only just started playing hide-and-seek in the house, and when they went somewhere fun, they would stand in line for hours—like the theme park, for instance—where by the end so much ice cream and so many rides on the carousel made them have to throw up. He remembers their regular breathing and their little baby hands balled into fists, which opened by reflex the second you touched them, he remembers their hair, their skin. And he believes he can even smell them. They smelled like warm milk. That alone comforted him: they were doing fine.

That was all he needed to know.

The programmed part of the night has come to a close. The blind grandfather has nodded off. And they are just getting ready to stand up, to give one final toast, when Sakura—in a wheelchair after all, because otherwise she would not have been able to go from table to table to greet her guests, ask whether they got enough to eat, enough to drink—suddenly stands up, not part of the protocol, and without introduction, without a segue, begins to read aloud from her book.

"What brings me joy," she reads. "When Father doesn't ask me any questions about the grade I got on my last test but only asks if I'd like some strawberries. Mother's knitting needles when she sets them to the side. They make an *X*. A bowl of rice with a plum in the middle. Knowing it will be sour before you even pop it into your mouth. The voices of the nurses when they're walking through the hallway. They say things like, 'Yesterday, I went to the movies.' The tree I can see from my window. It's so green now. My own private tree-movie-theater. Hiroshi's knock, and the way he opens the door, as quiet as the cat he smuggled into the room the last time he visited. My toenails. They aren't so bad after all. Fresh sheets. A bird in the tree, it's calling out, 'Spring,' and I call back, 'Summer.' The ventilator. White carnations. When Aunt Atsuko comes by for a little chat and can't stop talking about her back. I feel better afterward," and as suddenly as she started, she stops reading, coughs, bends over, says, coughing, "Thank you!"

And again: "Thank you! You prepared a celebration for us, which we would not have been able to pull off without you, and I will write down every last detail. Not here"—she points to the book—"but here"—to her heart—"the best place to preserve something, don't you think? When I was admitted to the hospital again for the fourth time in the span of four years, my first thought was: *This is it, then*. And on the one hand, it's true. This time around there is no chance of recovery, and it doesn't take long, not long at all, to give up hope.

"You cease to be a part of the world long before you've even left it, you lie inside while outside people are going about their lives. And in such a hurry! You have to wonder where they're all going. But on the other hand, and I don't really know if this is just another form of hopelessness, I have the feeling that I have just now started to live, as of a few months ago, and that death isn't my enemy but instead a friend who's coming to pick me up, and who is still allowing me the time I need to say goodbye, waiting patiently until I've finished, allowing me to linger, really. That's the truth.

"I would be happy to stay here a little longer, especially with you all, and I thought long and hard about whether it would be better if, for both our sakes, I kept up the illusion, held this in until it's all over, when I'm climbing back into the car and waving goodbye to you. Wouldn't it be better that way? But then the fact that I've prepared an end for her doesn't make her any less beautiful, does it? Will what was beautiful about this day remain, live on inside of us? In a way, it's like this wig I'm wearing. The second after I take it off is always terrifying. The slightest breeze feels so cold. And my head feels so strange. But then it all comes back to me. A warm tingling on my skin."

She takes it off.

"You see? The same Sakura! The game goes on, with or without it! One more roll of the dice. Then I reach the end."

Silence falls over everything for a moment. Nobody moves, and the applause only starts up with the help of the tables. Cautious at first, then louder and louder, until everyone is clapping. Only the grandfather remains undisturbed. His head hangs heavy over his sauce-flecked chest.

CHAPTER TWENTY-SIX

I nsanity!" Mie sinks into one of the chairs. "I don't know about you, but I need something stronger than champagne. A whiskey, please!"

They are in a bar not far from the chapel where they all cheered on the bride and groom one last time, no longer bound to their roles, but that didn't mean they were any less compassionate, just more exhausted than they might have been otherwise. And he feels a little sorry about his role as the boss, he would have very much liked to have given his colleagues another friendly pat on the shoulder, told them he'll make a deal, Monday morning they can come in at half past eight, the upcoming project requires their full attention. Yes, he had been close to saying that in spite of himself, but they would have probably just fallen into an uncomfortable silence, too tired to laugh about it.

"This exhaustion, you want to know where it's from, do you?" Mie rolls her eyes. "I have no idea. And it doesn't matter. We're tired. Period. More questions doesn't equal more answers. And I hate to say it, but you have too many questions. It would be nice if we could just sit here, if it's all right with you, without some long drawn-out conversation."

And so they sit there in their chairs, staring absentmindedly at the ice cubes melting in their glasses. His left foot is stroking her right one. Two pairs of shoes, facing each other. Whoever sees them, he thinks idly, would take her for his mistress. A woman who is finally realizing he is never going to get divorced and is sad about it, even though she knew it all along. Her sadness will last two or three months, four max, and then in the end she will untangle herself from him, without anything she did or said having made a difference.

He yawns. Thinks briefly about tomorrow. Maybe he'll finally go see Itō? He lives only one train station closer to the city after all, and it wouldn't be strange if he happened to—

"I'm backing out," says Mie.

"But we're not even close yet."

He is confused, because in his mind he was still sitting in the train on the way to Itō's, asking himself whether he should get off or if it would be better if he just kept going.

"I know. It's all very sudden for you. And I'm sorry, you did just climb aboard, and now what? After just three assignments? But if you're at all interested, here is the card for the agency that supplied most of the people there today. They're always looking for people, and especially—I'm sure about this—people around your age. You have—"

"But what are you saying?"

Once, he sat down in the wrong train, and it took a second before he realized after looking up from his paper. It was like he had landed in a parallel universe, and he was rattled by the tiered rice fields, one after the next, which appeared out the window instead of skyscrapers, rattled by the way they gleamed in the sunlight.

"But it's your dream! You said so yourself!" He is practically shouting. "It is your dream to be one of the best! And you had assignments lined up, a lot of them!"

"I gave those up."

"But why?"

Suddenly, he is wide awake. No trace of his earlier exhaustion. His foot was back on the ground. Hers too. Two pairs of shoes, facing away from each other.

"I made a decision. It has something to do with Sayuri. Remember her? The dead girl? I shouldn't have been allowed to play her. Rule number six: We don't make exceptions." A weak smile. She had come up with these rules just for his sake. In reality, there are none.

"But it doesn't matter . . ."

"It does matter! You've been saying that far too much tonight."

"Twice?"

"That's a lot."

"Doesn't matter. When I turned up in my pantsuit, I knew it was wrong to have come in the first place, but it was too late to turn back. The parents were already waving me inside and were elated to see me again. I could tell that they had stayed up the whole night before, unable to think of anything except their daughter's upcoming visit, the daughter they had convinced themselves had only left temporarily. A quick walk around the block, and now I was back. And that despite the fact that that wasn't what we had agreed on. Talking with each other while we held hands, sure! But out of grief, not because we were happy to see each other again. But I was powerless, you understand?

I had been sucked in. And there were my plush slippers with floppy bunny ears.

"The first thing they did was show me her bedroom. All pink everything, with posters of pop stars nobody knows anymore, and I don't know why I played along, probably out of sympathy. Stupid. Or maybe a sense of obligation? At any rate, they asked me to get in bed so they could watch me sleep awhile. And it was a child's bed, too short, filled with stuffed animals, but it doesn't matter—okay, you're right, it does matter—as soon as my head hit the pillow, I felt very tired, it was so cool and soft, and they said, 'Shh,' and covered me up, then again, 'Shh,' and then they stroked my cheeks until I really did fall asleep.

"And the funny thing was I slept great! Woke up refreshed, craving juice! And sweets! It wasn't magic, nothing supernatural, but for a few moments, I had transformed into Sayuri, a slightly chubby fourteen-year-old, who—nobody could get her to stop—walked around with headphones on from morning until night. That was why she never returned from that walk around the block. She didn't hear it coming. The train. And I was happy to have a family, happy to be at home. I would have loved, even though it quickly became too small, to have stayed lying in bed or gone into the living room. Would have watched TV while Mother cooked. Ate my dinner across from her and Father. Told them about my day. Then said good night. Stayed up doing homework for a bit. Written in my journal. Kissed my posters. The kinds of things you do when there's no one and nothing else that needs you and you know there's someone who cares about you and will turn off the light when you go to sleep."

"And? Did you stay in bed?"

"No, of course not. But maybe it was that nap? Maybe I slept too long or too deeply? Since then, all these memories have been flooding in, and no, you're wrong, I'm not too young to have any. I'm thirty years old."

He would have guessed younger.

"Thank you. Another whiskey, please!" She snaps her fingers.

"People only do that in movies," he says.

"I know," she laughs. "I wanted to try it."

It was the *shh* that made her decide, and realizing how much she actually needed that in her life. Doesn't he need that too, once in a while? He thinks of the cabdriver shakes his head.

"No."

"No? Honestly? I find that odd."

He should have said yes. But the *shh*—he returns to her point—can't be the only reason she's giving up, he insists. That's not something you jeopardize your career over. After all: twelve employees! He includes himself in that number. She has, he doesn't want to sound old-fashioned, but she does have a certain responsibility, although responsibility, he wants to make it clear, he doesn't consider to be old-fashioned at all, but, the word finally occurs to him—he means it's the *respectable* thing to do.

"Respectable? Well, as far as that goes, it's not something our industry is exactly known for. We're free spirits. Yourself included. Well, you a little less, maybe. But the others will manage; anyway, it was just one of their many gigs, not their bread and butter, and as far as my career is concerned"—she takes a generous gulp and wipes her mouth with the back of her hand—"I'll trade it for the memories. I have to go back first, and then maybe, who knows, things will start moving forward and I'll start all over. And then maybe you'll hear from me. A call when you're no longer expecting it? When you're sitting with your wife over dinner and . . . Not funny, you say? So then: one call late at night when she's fast asleep, and I will let you know whether it was worth it?"

"But go where? Back where?" He doesn't understand a word that's come out of her mouth. If she could please speak more plainly? Could he expect that much from her, at least? "You walk into my life, you step out of the shadow of a tree, and now you want to turn around in the middle of where I followed you to, and all you can offer me are riddles? I mean, who are you?" Leaning forward, he tosses her the question like a ball, but she doesn't catch it, so it falls to the ground, rolls away, comes to a stop somewhere. "Answer me, damn it! Who are you?"

Someone coughs. Someone is smoking at the bar. Thick clouds of smoke make their way over. The pianist, who had paused, starts up again. Most likely a part-timer who plays for drinks, he plunks out a meaningless tune that's so flat, he would love nothing more than to slam the piano lid down on his fingers—it's as flat, he thinks, as the feeling that will spread through him, as soon as Mie has gone back, to a place he can't picture—is it even a place that she's talking about or just the shadow she stepped out of and is now stepping back into?

"Fine! I'll tell you. My name"—and she squirms as she says this—"well, it's not important. For you it stays Mie. And Mie is . . ."

"I'm listening."

"A disgustingly normal wife. Too bad, hmm? I would have

liked to give you something different, some kind of calamity, something that can't be undone, like an abortion, or a tattoo in a place too intimate for me to tell you about. But there isn't anything! You understand? No secret to be uncovered. I am as normal as—let's say—that woman over there."

And he follows her nod, sees a woman who is reapplying her makeup and at the same time chatting incessantly with her friend, he can make out the words: "If I was you, I'd try out aquabics."

Words she utters without conviction, and the way she says them is like the perfume she's spraying generously onto her neck. A wet mist that settles, leaving only a hint of boredom.

"Disappointed?"

"No, not really." Because he doesn't believe her. Certainly a bluff, he thinks, she'll come out with the truth any moment.

But Mie has leaned back now. Says flatly, "I am."

And it takes a little while before she becomes recognizable to him again. She looks so crushed, as if she had just been woken from a dream.

"I wear sweatpants at home. And my favorite food is, no joke, mayonnaise. Sometimes I suck it out of a tube. It calms me down after a day of dealing with other peoples' drama. My husband finds it disgusting. But he sleeps with me anyway. Which happens every Friday and Saturday, and if I don't have a headache, then Sunday too. We're both too stressed to do it during the week. We turn the light out. He is the doctor. I am the patient. The roles are rarely reversed. And we say things like, 'Please get undressed.' And, 'But, Doctor, what's wrong with me?' And then he pulls out his instrument to, you know, examine me. I lie there waiting for some bad news, but then it's just that my 'breasts are too big,' so he massages that away. Too intimate. Yes, I know, but it's to replace the tattoo I don't have.

"When we're done, we turn the light back on, and I pass him the toilet paper roll that's under the bed, he passes it back to me. Then we read, he reads crime novels, I read romance novels, while we snack on some nuts, salty for him, caramelized for me, cracking away as we turn the pages. It's a nice feeling. That I'll admit. And yet, it's too bad. Don't you think? We might have a little more of it, just to imagine for a moment, if we were two unhappy lovers who met like this just once a year in a love hotel, always on the same day, because it is the day they happened to accidentally trip over each other's feet at the intersection in Shibuya.

"He is married, so is she. Three or four children involved. And they talk about driving away, about setting off without a destination in mind, about getting into a car and escaping it all. They see their suitcases in front of them. Cold headlights. Slapping. Kissing. The red light that makes them hit the gas, roads branching out before them. And somewhere, they come to a stop, get a coffee from the vending machine, take turns taking sips to brace themselves for the darkness ahead. An odyssey. It's my favorite fantasy.

"But I'll repeat, there is nothing. Too much nothing, you think? And this part is true as well: I wouldn't want it any other way. My husband is wonderful, maybe a little too wonderful. He's good-looking, and to top it all off, he takes care of my finances too. Gets so upset when I hand him all my bills in a shoebox, all jumbled up, of course—why can't I be like any other reasonable person and—and at this point he always starts to laugh. What is he talking about? Reason? When really I'm the one he should be talking about, his 'jungle bride.' It's a nickname, I like it. I prefer it to the usual 'you.' And I don't know if it's because of that or because of the way he smells when he comes into the bedroom on a Friday night after his shower—I'm already waiting for him, covers pulled up to my chin—and this is maybe a little unhealthy, but I would die if anything happened to him. A little scratch, and I wouldn't die immediately, sure—this is bad, isn't it?—but then I would feel the same pain as he did, at least almost the same, and I would scream, that's how much it would hurt, I would scream for and instead of him, and louder than him at that."

"Another whiskey, please!" This time, he is the one snapping his fingers.

"But they only do that in the movies," Mie says, taking off her shoes. See-through stockings. The bar has gotten packed in the meantime. More and more people are squeezing past them, and they have pushed a few chairs off to the side, to the back of the room, to make room for a dance floor. The pianist whips out something a little more spirited, but no one is dancing yet, it's still too early, and he falls back into his party tune, seems satisfied with that.

"Third rate, if you ask me."

"It is, isn't it?" Mie goes back to herself: "Third rate. A marriage like it came out of a picture book, and at every page someone points and thinks how boring it looks! Wishes for something a little more exciting. A whirlpool next to the bed, the love hotel scene continues to unfold, following the two unhappy people wherever they go, with different names, different pasts, in the hope of finally arriving somewhere. They are always on the road, moving from place to place, only to end up right back where they started. They call so they can hear the voices of the children they left behind. Hang up as soon as they say hello.

"Again, just something I think about Friday nights when I can't sleep. My husband already snoozing beside me. The toilet paper roll back in its spot under the bed. And don't you think it's strange? That I need this? This fantasy of being unhappy? To tell you the truth, I'm always working on it in my mind. Contemplating different beginnings and endings and as many middles as you can imagine. I have enough to fill a whole diorama series, and yes, I have at least one finished version in my head. Twelve episodes, and each more tearful than the next! And all while I'm lying next to my husband, whose back reminds me of a mountain range, so quiet and peaceful, spread out under the dark night sky.

"I'm kind of addicted to it. Which is probably why I like playing aunt and sister. My husband doesn't find it as disgusting as the mayonnaise tube, at least. He says he finds it a little odd, but somehow—oh, I just love him!—morally justifiable."

CHAPTER TWENTY-SEVEN

He still believes she's bluffing. She must be, he thinks. All of this can't be true. He looks back at the woman chatting with her friend. She keeps glancing at her fingernails. Then back at her phone. It's buzzing. Could she just excuse her for a second, just one second? It's the guy, she knows the one she's talking about, the one with oiled hair from bowling. "It's probably about last time," she says, looking back at her fingernails. "You know what I'm talking about." Her friend nods conspiratorially.

"But," he tries now to find a way back into the conversation. "What is so bad and strange about it? You love him. And he loves you. Isn't that exactly how it should be?"

Mie whimpers.

"Of course, but. Okay, this is what's messed up about it: when I work as a stand-in, at least part of me gets a deep satisfaction that I don't get out of my everyday life, probably because I always have one foot out the door. I always feel like something's going to happen. But then nothing does. More nothing. Like really early on"—she tries to laugh—"I toyed with the idea of not telling my husband about the agency, and not because he wouldn't approve—he's not that kind of guy, thankfully, otherwise, we wouldn't be together—but because I got a thrill out of the possibility that—just think—he could call me up one day and hire me as his wife. And there you have it: that's what's messed up!

"I need to get out before it's too late. Because it's true what people say: everything is good between us. We might argue sometimes, sure, but never to the point of breaking. I've tried that. It's hopeless. Once I was even holding a plate, and all I wanted was to throw it against the wall as hard as I possibly could, but then, diorama or not, that felt cheap, and I still remember thinking how embarrassing it would be if I missed. And there would be so much glass everywhere! And what if I missed some? Because the shards are so tiny you can hardly see them, but they still hurt so much if someone steps on them? An heirloom too. Beautifully made. And I'm glad I managed to pull myself together. I put the plate down.

"Instead, I threw a tomato. Not that smart, either. That mess! Just from a tomato! You wouldn't believe how much juice is in there. In any case, that was a lesson for me. So much juice in something so small. Not something..." She takes a deep breath. "Not something you want to make a mess of."

The woman at the next table is still on the phone. She's drumming on the table with her fingernails. Her friend hisses intermittently: she shouldn't give a damn about his fairy tales, it's probably the same thing he tells everybody. But the woman seems to be enjoying them. She laughs more than once, her laughter like a coo, she stops drumming a few times to run her hand through her hair. "He's lying!" hisses her friend, but she doesn't get through.

"You said you want to go back?"

"Hmm, I said that?" Mie purses her lips. Looks up at the ceiling bashfully.

"And that the memories would torment you and were the reason you wanted to go back to the beginning?"

"Oh right, yes. I might have laid it on a little thick. See? Acting isn't so easy to quit. I meant 'back' in the sense of—well, what the heck? Here's a quick, a really quick story. A drama, so to speak, the only thing in my life that, I promise you, I will be thankful for from today. Namely, it has to do with my mother, who I had a falling-out with a few years ago—again, totally boring—and believe it or not, I can't for the life of me remember what it was about. I forgot. Maybe because of the tattoo I wanted to get back then? That could have been it. I can't think of what else it could be. Pretty stupid, right? Especially when you consider that I didn't end up getting it because I'm terrified of pain, even just a pinch.

"Anyway. Mother has earned an apology from me, and I'll bet she'll be happy when I'm suddenly standing at her door and my hair isn't bleached anymore, which might also have been one of the reasons we fought. I already know what she's going to say, which is that it always stops raining at some point, and the sun always comes out again in the end. And she'll go, 'Shh,' because I'll have started crying by then, and she'll fry me the thickest, fluffiest okonomiyaki with lots of mayonnaise on top.

"So there it is. And that would be the end of it. One more banality for me to get over. Not so bad. Not strange. Just a bit of a shame how predictable it is. Just a straight road without any bends. Only the precipice stays the same, remember?"

He thinks of his own mother, the one presumed dead, whom

he went to visit in the nursing home after learning she was still alive, only for her to pretend she couldn't remember anything anymore, although according to her team of staff he asked later, she definitely did not have dementia and, on the contrary, used to entertain them with all her tales of former lovers.

Everyone was very surprised to learn she had a son. She had never mentioned him. She did, on the other hand, bring up the cats she couldn't take with her to the nursing home, and quite frequently at that. She asked after them day after day. But that's how it is with old people. Some grow forgetful, others don't, and everyone constructs their past in their own way, deleting this and inventing that, painting over certain details however they see fit. At this, he went back into her room to look at her face, because he knew he would never see her again.

And remembering now, he's amazed the only thing he noticed was the red lipstick on her yellow teeth when she smiled, telling him that she would like to take a little afternoon snooze, and would he be so kind as to close the door quietly on his way out? The rest is a blur. He couldn't describe it if he tried. The composite sketch that came out of all this would amount to a grossly inadequate reconstruction, worthless in proving they were related at all.

Whatever was behind the great bluff never came to light, and he can't help but feel like something's been withheld from him. Mie, so proper sitting here now, may only have wanted to spare him the truth. He wouldn't put it past her. And he almost wishes she had. Lied to him. Her story doesn't seem to fit her somehow. A bird of paradise with a cane. But then—he thinks of her snacking on nuts while she lies in bed reading, next to her husband who smells of soap and water—he really does hope she was telling the truth, and that it's just the whiskey that went to his head. Everything's spinning. A vortex.

In his mind, he's the one lying next to her, and he reaches over to make sure she is flesh and blood, the blanket rippling gently, the sheet slipping away, he wraps around her like a drowning man who still believes he will be rescued, thrashes about one more time before he dives down, very slowly, and she slips down with him. And for a moment he doesn't think it's out of the realm of possibility, so he opens his mouth to suggest it: Should they go find a hotel? Or better yet, just drive away? Right now? Should they just drive away from it all?

It wouldn't be a script. Just life. His life. Hers. But halfway through the thought, she's already slipping her shoes back on, and he can see that they're a perfect fit. Everyone on earth has his slippers, he thinks fleetingly. And how supple they become over time! He shuts his mouth. Completely impossible. Driving somewhere? Where would they go? He laughs wearily to himself. Without a driver's license?

"What do you think?" Mie is standing up, she's swaying a little. "Should we dance?" And as he starts to object: "Oh, come on already!" She takes him by the hand, pulling him up with one tug, and stumbles with him through the smoky, sweaty crowd to the dance floor, where next they just stand without moving, then put their arms a little clumsily around each other.

Someone yells, or maybe he whispers it himself: "A little more oomph!" And the pianist does his best, halting mid-song and switching to another one. "As Time Goes By." He recognizes it instantly, after just the first stroke. He pulled it off the shelf—when was that, exactly? Yesterday? A week ago? And why?—and then pushed it right back in again. And he wants to tell her about it as they gradually find their footing, but she has laid her head on his shoulder, and it's difficult to talk about something when he doesn't quite know what it means himself.

"You're a fool," he says instead.

She lifts her head: "So are you."

They keep dancing. They are alone on the dance floor, and the people who were watching them initially soon turn away, so he relaxes a bit. Nobody is paying them any attention as they stumble around, glued to their spot on the floor, and when it's over, they both stay standing there, waiting for the next song. Forward and back. Right, left. Once they turn. But after that they stick to smaller moves, which don't throw them off track. Doesn't he have to go home? To his wife?

He says, "It's fine, it's fine, it's fine."

"But, Mr Katō!"

For a moment, he thinks she means someone else.

PART
THREE

PART
THREE

CHAPTER TWENTY-EIGHT

The bike fell over. As his heavily pregnant daughter stands in the doorway, rain-soaked and looking very much like him, with her eyes that are a little too deep set, cast down at the doormat, that is his first thought, and that he could have prevented it if he had just gone back to the mice, but his wife had waved, and, well, he could have predicted this would happen.

"What happened?" he declares more than asks, and when she doesn't answer: "You should have brought an umbrella. But that's all right. Come in."

She has a gym bag over her shoulder, its strap is cutting into her skin, and judging by its weight when he takes it from her, she must have been rushing and thrown in only the most unnecessary things—a hair straightener, he guesses, three pairs of shoes, and nail polish. If only his wife were here! But she is at the gym, and he wonders what she would do if she were in his shoes. Give her a hug? Perhaps. Make her a cup of tea?

At a loss, he trudges into the kitchen ahead of her, she hasn't yet said a word, and so he looks for the kettle, there it is, and for the tea bags. "Where could they be?"

The daughter points silently to the closet behind him.

"Oh yes, right. Now what?"

She points to the faucet.

"How much water? Is that good?"

She nods.

The sound of the gas stove as he turns it on, the flames flicker up briefly, but then he releases the switch too soon and the fire goes out.

"Is it broken?" He tries again. Presses in, holds it down, lets go. "It's broken!"

And she tries to stifle a laugh. He hears it. She's chuckling.

"You're so funny," she finally lets out. "Look, like this." She shows him how. "Poor Mom! She can never leave you alone."

"Okay, okay, it's not that bad. I'm alive, aren't I?"

"I don't know how it's possible!" She rinses out two mugs. "That someone can live without ever making themselves a cup of tea. But thanks anyhow." She smiles. "You tried your best."

"All just a show," he smiles back, "to cheer you up a bit."

But she doesn't buy it. The kettle starts whistling. She pours the water into the mugs. "Five minutes." He glances at the clock. His wife, he thinks, would have already found out everything there was to know, like why had their daughter driven across the country so soon before the birth? And without telling anyone in advance? It surely wasn't homesickness, or was it? It was possible. He looks at her stomach.

"It suits you," he says.

"You think? Really?" She pushes it forward. "The little guy's been growing like crazy recently. The midwife says he's a big one and that it's not going to be easy to get him out. And the way he kicks. Here, feel it!" She puts his hand on her side. "Can you feel it? No?"

"Yes, now I can."

And when he looks up at her tender face, he sees tears rolling down her cheeks, and he reaches for the dish towel, the one full of stains, and holds it out to her.

"First drink your tea. Then we'll talk. Nothing," he says, "is as bad as it seems right now."

His wife, he's certain, would have said something similar, and he desperately wishes she would get back before they finish their tea. Does her husband know she's here?

"No."

She drains the tea bags and tosses them a little too vigorously into the trash can, snapping it shut noisily and whacking the lid with her palm after it's closed. But he can figure it out—that is, if he ever takes a second to actually think.

"Have some tea first," he repeats. That's all he can think to say.

Next scene. Same place. When his wife comes inside, noticeably late, he notes—the rain held her up, she calls from the entryway, she had to wait for half an hour under the vegetable stand—the daughter springs to her feet and, before she can even manage a sound of surprise, throws herself into her arms, sobbing.

What happened? He asked the very same question, he thinks. And he hears them talking in the hallway, words and phrases that could just as easily have been on TV: an argument. *But about what?* The mother-in-law. *Oh, her.* And he hadn't tried to see her side of it. *Typical.* And then she called him a coward, and he went and spent the whole night out drinking with his buddies, came home piss drunk, and she lost her nerve. *That's understandable.*

She doesn't have any more patience. And country living on top of it. And with the baby coming, how are they supposed to manage it all?

Oh, hush now! There, there. That all sounds terrible. Her hands are so cold. Could she make her some tea? Maybe draw her a bath? Then everything will become more clear.

Essentially the same thing he said, her *And why was this?* just sounded so much more comforting. And he feels like he's been pushed into the corner, even though this is what he wanted, he kept running to the window to wait for her to finally come around the bend. He was ready to call her, but what's the point of her having a phone if she never turns it on? He was sure he wouldn't be able to reach her, like so many times before.

He silently cursed the whole dancing business, he blamed the instructor, and in the end, it was the daughter who had to calm him down because he couldn't sit still anymore, he couldn't control himself, he even said out loud that he had known nothing good would come of hopping around.

"Now, Dad, I beg you: Who is hopping around here? The only person I see hopping around is you! I'm sure she'll be here soon. It's the weather! And the path up here is also so steep."

She can't believe her mother does this to herself. At her age. If she were her, she would have moved down years ago. But that was her opinion and no, Mom had never said that, that's just how good her imagination is, it's not exactly fun lugging the groceries all the way up here; if they at least had a car!

"But neither of you ever wanted one. Which means, Mom probably did. She crammed so much for the driving test only to have it fall through so suddenly, and then she didn't want to try again and gave up instead. Kind of tragic, don't you think?"

And he had opened his mouth to protest, but what she was saying was true, and also, what she couldn't know was that he had been secretly pleased with how quickly the subject of a car was taken off the table, so he hurried to present her with the advantages of the house instead, pointing out, among other things, how far they could see in every direction, perfect for the fireworks, for instance—you can't put a price on that.

"But the fireworks only happen once a year," she reminded him. And at that moment, the door opens. "Finally," he grumbles. Now mother and daughter are in the bathroom. He hears them laughing. Wow, can he kick! Do they already have a name picked out? Yes, and it's . . . Running water. He catches the first syllable in time. A bright *A*.

"It will all work out, just you watch." His wife has tied on her apron. "You'll see in a few days. It is their first child after all. It puts people a little on edge."

He thinks about the intersection. And the way he held her, gently at first, but then, because she would not stop crying, more tightly, a little rougher out of an urge to cause her pain that he felt so ashamed of afterward, and she freed herself from his arms, crying, and ran away from him. He ran after her through the pouring rain, the whole thing becoming more and more of a chase, where it was no longer just a matter of catching her, but—he paused—fell behind on purpose. Gave her a good ten meters' head start. Dropped even farther back. Let her go.

He didn't catch up until the playground, a sad rectangle with nothing but a squeaky swing set and rusty slide, but by then, she'd calmed down and was crouched in the gravel, her hands cupped protectively over her bulging belly, clearly waiting for him to yell at her, though he wouldn't. Why had he let her go? It was a game after all, he whispered. Not to her? It was, it was. The rain slowly let up. And they sat for a while between the swings and the slide, too exhausted and too frightened to go directly home.

"So much open space," his wife had said when they finally rose to their feet. "They should have dancing here."

To which he had replied: "You and all your ideas! You wouldn't even be against dancing in a graveyard."

His thoughts returned to the present. "And our son-in-law? Someone has to let him know."

"I know. Would you be so kind?" She cracks three eggs.

"What? Me? Why me?"

"Tell him she doesn't mean it. It's just a little disagreement. Tell him it's actually a good thing they're getting this out before the baby arrives. It clears the air. And please be friendly. No need for a lecture. The situation is delicate enough as it is."

Like he would do such a thing! But she is already taking the chopped ginger out of the freezer, so he has no choice but to go to the phone, a device that makes him nervous—it makes him think of his office and how natural the phone seemed there on his desk compared to here at home, where there are so many unknowns—he can't see to the right or left of him, only straight ahead, at nothing. And he dials the number his wife taped below the keys, and says, "Hello? It's . . . Everything's fine, no need to worry. She's just taking a bath. No, not a bit, you know that. It's the hormones, they're going haywire. Oh, it will all work out," and more to that end, and it strikes him that someone else is speaking for him, when inside he's saying instead, "It's not going to work out."

CHAPTER TWENTY-NINE

It's just like old times." From the kitchen comes the smell of freshly steamed dumplings. "Some things never change. Like this smell." The daughter sniffs the air. "It reminds me of home no matter where I am, and sometimes I even dream about it. It's a nice dream. Everyone's in their spot at the table. Mom is here, I'm there, and"—does he know how the brother is doing? No, he doesn't know. Good, he thinks.

"Bad!" his wife yells. But he is on the road to recovery. "The flu." It did a number on him, he lost five kilos, and he was already slight to begin with. But the delicate ones are naturally tougher. The daughter-in-law has her hands full nursing him back to health. "And you know"—she brings in a tray of assorted sauces—"she's not doing all that great herself, poor thing. It just doesn't seem to want to work out for her." At her age—how old is she again? Thirty-eight? Thirty-nine?—her biological clock simply has other ideas.

"You know who you're talking to, right?" The daughter dishes up her plate. "I happen to be an expert in that field." And as she starts to eat, she explains which procedures she's had to undergo, she talks about ovaries, amniotic sacs, and mucous membranes, and he turns the TV up a little, there's a commercial on for shampoo that prevents hair loss, and the man using it already noticed a difference in the second week, any earlier and he would have been exaggerating, and there's a graph showing a steady curve to prove it. "Hard to believe, but true!" It's followed by a toothpaste commercial. Not all that appetizing, either. And then he hears his daughter again, she is really hitting her stride. The guilt was the worst part. Over time, she began to feel like a failure. And why? Because of two cysts you couldn't see were there, but—

He is only half listening, turns back to the TV. MAXX deodorant is odor-free, guaranteed. And not only that, but roughly 63 percent of users can confirm: you sweat about a third less. His wife exclaims over and over again, "That can't be!" And keeps saying how happy she is. A happy ending after all. Now if only the brother . . . How wonderful that would be! Each of them holding a baby when they're all together at New Year's.

And then they move on to other topics, chatting about the neighbors who flew to Australia for five days last summer as a family. What if they did that sometime? Definitely. But not Australia. Her husband has a fear of flying. *Really, still?* Yes, and nothing can be done about it, "because at the end of the day it's irrational. I mean, he knows it's one of the safest modes of transportation there is. He knows the statistics. Still. What can you do? Fear can't be rationalized away." It's quite possible it will go away on its own one day, but until then they just need to be patient. "And what about you, Dad?"

He jumps.

"Didn't you want to cart Mom off to France? That was your plan anyway. Remember? We were all here around the table. You were over there. And we were playing a game, some kind of dice game," and he had pulled the card *Lifelong Dream*. And he had stood up and started talking about Paris "so animatedly I can still picture it now. About walking with Mom through the city. *Holding ice cream cones,* you said, which is probably why this still stands out in my mind. Because you were pacing back and forth with your arm in the air like you had it around Mom, and we were all laughing so hard, remember? Because your ice cream fell on the ground? And you tried to pick it up but it kept slipping, so you couldn't? And by then it had all completely melted?"

No, strange. He doesn't remember.

His wife says, "I do. The game was called *Tell Me Something,* and you were really good at it. Wasn't he?" She turns to the daughter. "When there's anything with acting involved, Dad is second to none." Maybe she would look for it again, it was that blue game board with the clouds, it must be here somewhere, she can see it clearly in front of her. And it would be interesting to check, she says, *interesting* in the sense of "revealing," and see how different their answers would be to exactly the same questions if they played it again after all these years. "Very interesting," she adds.

He changes the channel. Commercials again.

He went to bed a little earlier than usual. He was worn out from so much conversation, for so much of which he had just sat there silently, and at any rate, his being there didn't seem to be all that important, which was a way to say without saying—except he says it into the darkness anyway—he was bothering them. He could tell by how they relaxed when he left the room. His wife leaned back in her seat. His daughter stretched out her legs. And the *good night* they called after him was the *good night* you would say to a guest whose departure you were looking forward to because it meant you could finally be yourself again.

Since when had they slept in separate rooms? And why? Oh, it just happened over time, because she snores so loudly he can't sleep a wink (a lie), but apart from that, the daughter will understand this too someday, marriage isn't about the bed you share, but what you learn about each other outside of it.

"Take your father and I, for instance. We're actually quite similar."

"Oh? In what way?"

But at that point, he had already pulled the door shut behind him, and the whispering that was still audible from the top step stayed outside it. Every now and then, a laugh filters through as if from far away, or a stray word or two makes its way up to his ear, but given how quiet it is, it could just as easily have been his breath, which he is holding, then letting out in bursts, as if he has something he'd like to say. That he had been to the travel agency only yesterday, for instance, to collect some "preliminary information," as he cautiously put it. And that the clerk had printed out a list of flights for him and highlighted the cheapest, and he asked her whether the prices also included cancellation insurance, because you never know. Then he thanked her for her time and effort. He would come back once they decided on a date.

"No problem," she said. And he could be certain about this, at least: "Paris will be waiting." Truly a spectacular city! She had never been, but the friend of a friend had just come back from vacationing there and was swept completely off her feet, especially by the Louvre. It sounds huge! Yes, that it is. Oh, he's familiar?

And they launched into a conversation where her friend's words blended with his, mingling in a pleasant way. The travel agent seemed pleased that something came along to help pass the time until her lunch break, because, as he could surely see, she sighed, travel agencies aren't what they used to be. Most people use the internet to book things now. And she often feels superfluous now, "like I might as well be a cardboard cutout. Someone just looking through the window wouldn't be able to tell the difference."

CHAPTER THIRTY

He stuck the list of flights between the pages of the travel guide. He'll look into it as soon as everything with the daughter has been worked out, so two or three days from now; he is sure she'll stay for at least that long, although now that she's here, he thinks she should stay for at least a week. Meet up with old friends, go shopping, have a spa day, let someone else cook for her. Get a facial! Take as much time as she needs. And yes, he supposes that's another thing to consider—moving the birth here, home; he would bet the medical care here in the suburbs is head and shoulders above what she gets out in the country, and it's a matter of safety after all, both the daughter's and their future grandson's.

He'll work this into conversation tomorrow at breakfast, as delicately as possible. For now, he lies in the dark, waiting for a sound. There! A creak! The old bed slats. He can tell immediately it's his daughter, not his wife. She would sound different. Yes, definitely. His wife probably took the guest room tonight because of how cold and drafty it is—not suitable for a pregnant woman—and he runs his hand back and forth along the wall, wondering whether he should reserve a double or a twin for Paris.

Two single rooms would probably be too much in comparison. He will miss the wall. The rough wallpaper. And one last thought before sleep overtakes him: "But I'm the one who snores, not her." At least that was his wife's basis for moving into the room the daughter is in now a good five years ago. Was she telling the truth? One more last thought. He has never heard himself snore.

"Back so soon? But you just got here yest—"

"I know. And I'm sorry. I'm causing such a commotion. But I was able to get some clarity last night, and that was worth coming all the way here for. When it comes down to it, it doesn't make much of a difference whether I leave today or tomorrow. Anyway, we'll see each other very soon. You'll visit as soon as he's born, won't you? Mom said she would be happy to stay a little longer too." Could he spare her? Now that he knows how to operate the stove? "And how about"—she leans in to whisper—"you start making her tea for a change once in a while, or better yet, what if you bought her flowers? Something nice? Do it for me! And don't worry, you'll still be the man of the house, that's not going to change," she says with added silliness. "By the way, I learned some new things about you I had no idea about, like that you wrote poetry?" She would like to read it someday. Her gym bag is already over her shoulder. No, they don't have to walk her to the station. She can manage on her own.

His wife, who has just stumbled in, quickly presses a lunchbox into her hands. "All your favorites. Except the pickled veggies turned out a little too sour for my taste, the cucumbers especially." The daughter looks up at the house. Couldn't they just? At least a little way? As far as the deserted patch of land?

Please, no, she is no longer a child. Her chin is trembling ever so slightly. "Everything was wonderful." And then she turns to him. "And you're right. Why move back down when you're still able to make it up here? And the view really is price-less," she says. Before the road bends and disappears from view, she turns around again and waves. Then she's off down the hill.

He sighs.

"Commotion indeed!"

His wife sighs as well. Bends down to pull up a tuft of grass growing between the slabs of pavement leading up to the house; the joints still need to be cleaned thoroughly. Maybe it would be worth filling them with sand. Nothing else has worked. She shakes the earth loose from the roots.

"Look how thick they are!"

And they sigh again, at the same time this time, both of them looking alternately at the roots and the bend in the road. The air, it seems, smells particularly delicious today.

"It's from the rain," she says and disappears into the house.

He has a long day ahead of him. He could visit Itō.

CHAPTER THIRTY-ONE

Entering the flower shop, he is hit head-on with the scent of damp soil, and he immediately feels lost, as if he's in a jungle, lush greenery grasping at him from all sides. A sign reads, "Aquatic and Climbing Plants," and another: "Warning! Carnivorous!" He glances around anxiously. Are there animals here too? He hears footsteps. Someone is approaching. His first impulse is to flee. But he's frozen. He can make out the shape of something moving in the undergrowth. And for a moment he believes it is crawling toward him, but then he sees it is a hose, nothing more than a yellow rubber hose the salesman is pulling behind him.

They specialize in exotic plants, he explains, his eyes lighting up, the orchids are in especially high demand right now. Is he looking for anything in particular?

"Yes, roses."

Oh, but roses are completely overrated, if he asks him. Wouldn't he instead... No? He insists? "Too bad." The salesman looks sadly back in the direction of the undergrowth. "We just received a delivery of the genus *Laelia*. Each one more magnificent than the last." Would he like to see? He would not. "All right, then, as you wish." He pushes past him to one of the frosted glass cases. "You can't go wrong with roses after all. A safe bet. For your wife, I assume?"

"Yes." He feels hot. "It's supposed to be a surprise." Would it be possible to have the flowers delivered? Just as is? Without a message? He speaks quickly to get this whole business over with—his hand has brushed against something sticky, a hairy leaf closing around a flesh-colored flower.

The salesman grins. "You got the idea from that TV show, right? I watch it too. And you wouldn't believe how many orders we've gotten since it aired, and always roses, of course! Because they were roses on the show, delivered without a message because they said that way it would leave more of an impression. Though, a gift is something so personal—don't you think it makes more sense to give it to the person directly?" But because he doesn't answer, hard-set on not engaging in conversation: "Red, correct? The usual!"

In the show, they explained red was the color of love, but if he can spare a minute—there is an entire language of color with its own myriad valences. Yellow stands for loyalty, white for— "But you did say you don't have much time, didn't you? I understand." He takes down the address. "It's all set. This afternoon between two and two thirty." And then he apologizes without explanation. "Please forgive me," the man says, not like a salesman but like someone who accidentally bumped into him in passing, in a tone that's remorseful but casual at the same time, and in a way that is unusual for him, he hastens to exit the store and get away from the salesman, as if he were jostled, it's too stuffy in here for him, the plants seem to smell almost putrid.

Only when he feels asphalt under his feet does he regain his senses. That's settled. He is filled with a dull satisfaction, and just as he's walking away, his heel already rolling, the ball of his foot almost in contact with the ground, when the salesman—what does he want now?—yanks open the door behind him.

"Your receipt. You forgot it."

"Oh, how silly of me!" He stuffs it into his pocket.

On the way to the train station, doubt starts to creep in. Should he have gone with the orchids? And what about white roses instead of red? Then he would be able to say that she deserved something special and out of the ordinary, except that he doesn't want to say anything, at least nothing that would require him to explain himself. Even one word would be one too many when his wife is dancing toward him, overcome with joy, and he can already imagine—his modesty. Why is she acting like this over a few flowers? She has a whole garden full of them.

He thinks of how it would overwhelm him too—his wife's quiet delight. But there is the homeless man. He greets him.

"Hello, how are you?" And he's disappointed when the old man on his cardboard doesn't reply, instead stares straight through him. "Didn't sleep well?" he tries again.

In vain.

The homeless man doesn't give more than a grunt in reply. He suddenly looks very old. For the first time, he notices gray stubble on his beard. Has that always been there? All those little blood vessels? And the bags under his eyes? He also notices that the box he is sitting on is completely soaked from yesterday's rain. Should he go find him a new one? They must have some at the supermarket.

"No." The homeless man slowly lifts his head. "It's pointless." He's peed himself. It happens to him a lot now, and he has no control over it; it rains, but not from the sky—this part he enjoys—instead, it's like he is the cloud. "By the time I get to my feet, it's already too late, so I just stay seated. More convenient that way. Don't you think?" He seems tired. "But this stays between us, hm?"

"Of course."

"Good, good. Not a word to your wife. She shouldn't get any ideas. But she already knows anyway that I've always been better than you!"

"It's true." But his voice sounds serious, too serious for these kinds of jokes, and he adds: "Mr Cloud!" which makes the homeless man laugh.

Now he's feeling sorry for bothering him in the first place, he should have let him piss in peace. Rule number seven, he thinks: We respect the silence of those who don't want to speak. They have their reasons. What would Mie have to say about that? He feels a pang in his chest. She disappeared from his life as suddenly as she appeared. Never got back in touch. Not after she led him off the dance floor into a cab, put some cash in his hand, and slammed the door behind him. He should go home. That's where he belongs.

In his imagination, Mie is with her mother, apologizing—not with her words but with her actions, by helping her out around the house a bit. Her gaze drifts over the objects scattered around—a massager shaped like a cat's paw, a magnifying glass, a small bottle of stomach pills—and she realizes how much time has passed since her last visit. This weighs on both of them as they quietly restore things to the way they used to be. And they manage to do it, if not entirely then enough so that the precipice they're tiptoeing over seems smaller. The sound of their footsteps on the tatami floor. It joins with her breathing, the distant ticking of a clock.

At this moment, he would very much like to be drinking black tea with lemon with her. Asking her if she doesn't miss it? Playing family? Please smile! He forces himself to. He actually did paint red dots on his toes.

CHAPTER THIRTY-TWO

Itō's house. It must be around the back. But instead of the house, he finds a bulldozed lot with wooden stakes hammered into the corners of the property.

Torn down?

He rings the neighbor's bell.

"Yes, just recently. A fire. Nothing could be saved."

"And what about Itō?"

"They moved in with some relatives. They're doing fine, as far as I know. Of course, it was a terrible shock. They lost everything. All those memories, all gone. They said the biggest loss was their photo albums and not having any more photos of the children. The rest they could deal with, they said. Awful, isn't it? Such dear people and then this! But happiness isn't guaranteed, it's here one minute and gone the next, and that's just life." And she nods as if what she said needed confirmation. "They returned one time. Late one night. I watched them from my window. They stood exactly where you were just a moment ago, looking at the house that wasn't there anymore, but they seemed to be able to see it anyway." It was a sight she wouldn't forget.

"And then?"

"They left. The husband was leaning on his wife. He was

already quite dependent on her, if you remember. Some disease. Something to do with his muscles." Or maybe it was the nerves? As his friend, he would certainly know more about it. She herself only witnessed it from afar. His growing weaker and weaker. "A motorcycle? No, I never heard anything about that!" But wait—yes, actually, years ago, "and he was always working on it. Every weekend and every night after he got home from work. And now that I think of it, I remember him saying, *I love getting my hands dirty,* and that once he was finished customizing it, he had grand plans.

"But then he got sick. You could hardly recognize him after that. He shuffled and had a bad limp. And at some point, they sold it. I still remember the way he cried talking about it." At least that's what she heard from the other neighbors. Also that he still managed to get out quite a bit, the retirement center organized regular bus trips, and they always brought something back from each excursion. "And they were very generous, let me tell you! Those peaches!" She indicates the size with her hands. "So juicy." She smacks her lips. Had he gotten any?

"Yes." He thinks back to the wrinkled skin. And about how they had laughed in the office, saying it looked like the backside of an old woman.

"Is everything all right?"

He has suddenly grown very pale. "Nothing, nothing. Just feeling a little nauseous is all." He probably just ate something that didn't agree with him.

"Could I get you some water? If you'd like to just wait a moment?"

No, he waves her off.

But he really doesn't look well at all. Just one glass? It won't take long.

"No!" he shouts. The neighbor flinches. "You were very helpful, thank you."

She watches him go, he can feel her eyes on the back of his neck, she watches until he has rounded the corner and stumbled into the first bush he sees, throwing up between the branches poking him in the face.

"All lies!" he hisses, and in his mind, he clings to the vision of Itō riding his motorcycle into the wind, which leaves him breathless, he sees him roaring into the setting sun, then skidding to a stop somewhere, setting up camp, lying under twinkling stars. And this scene seems to him to ring truer than what actually befell him, much truer; at this very moment he is on the adventure of his life.

If he happened to run into a colleague now and Itō were to come up, he would say, "What, you haven't heard? He is traveling all over. Incredible, isn't it? He gave us all the finger!" And he wouldn't allow a word of ridicule to cross anyone's lips, he would personally put his fist in the stomach of anyone who uttered the slightest laugh, punch him until he believed it. That Itō had driven far away from them all.

He has to drag himself up the mountain. Too much has robbed him of strength today. His daughter leaving—she walked down this way on her short little legs—but that was so long ago now! The flowers he bought his wife on her behalf, because he was disturbed by how little she expected of him. Itō's house, and the

fact that he had only been there once with his wife, years ago—
the four of them sat in the living room and drank coffee and
talked about their children, what they were worried about with
each of them, especially the sons, sons were more difficult than
daughters, even if it didn't appear that way at first. Then about
the advantages of suburban living. How fortunate they were to
have a house with a garden, it was a lot of work, but it was work
where afterward you could see exactly what you accomplished,
like with the freshly mowed lawn, for example.

The motorcycle was still just a fantasy at that point. And
when Itō started in on the subject—they were just praising the
delicious tarts, is that a hint of rum?—his wife disappeared into
the kitchen with a "Not again!" to get the recipe, which is when
he really got going, and for the better part of an hour, the Royal
Enfield was all he talked about, which is why they never went
back and only extended a half-hearted invitation on their part,
then left it at that single visit that had bored them to death.

When he next saw him in the office, he was brought back to
the living room and the fist-size hole in the wall he had stared
at while Itō was carrying on about how beautiful "his" *Enfield*
was—how had it gotten there in the first place? Maybe during
a fight? And couldn't they have covered it with a picture? And
he ended up avoiding him without really knowing why, feeling
a little sad about it, but not too much. The friendly tone they
had used with each other until then became increasingly polite,
but he blamed it on the age difference, which was laughable in
hindsight: Itō was ten years older than he was.

At that time, it seemed like half a century, today, he thinks
as he stops to catch his breath, like the split second that passes

when you glance away from someone. He is gasping for air. What on earth is the matter with him? He hasn't even reached the empty field yet. No bench. He eases himself onto the curb. A group of schoolchildren are marching up, hunched under their backpacks, singing an old nursery rhyme about the red dragonfly, which he had also learned in school years ago. So, they're still teaching it.

Does Grandpa need help? The biggest and strongest among them stations himself in front of him. The others hang back, nudging each other.

"No, you know what, I'm just having a little rest. The path is pretty steep. Just wait until you get to be my age. But you still have plenty of time before that happens. Here"—he takes a few coins from his pocket—"buy yourselves something sweet!"

"Thanks so much!"

And they are back on their way, heads huddled together, and he can hear them whispering about how best to divide the money, and whether they should save it, or if it would be better to spend it on some toffee. Then they strike up their singing again, their voices rising higher and higher. And at some point, he loses them, though he thinks he can still hear them singing about how much they miss the twilight, and about the nurse-maid who left them behind.

He heaves himself up with a jerk. *Up to the field,* he thinks, *I can do it.*

"What brings me joy . . ." He is surprised when these words come out of his mouth; he pushes out one after the other every meter he walks, as if, in a way, they are helping to pull him up: "Coming home. The smell of food. Sliding into my slippers, remembering my father. That creaky floorboard in the hallway that we won't get fixed. My wife, when I explain that the creaking comes from the wood as it shifts. And how amazed she is, or at least pretends to be, that it's alive." And he is already tipping the hat he isn't wearing, placating the mice. The handlebars of the bicycle are jutting out of the grass like an arm. "And once more from the top," he gasps, dragging himself past it: "What brings me joy."

CHAPTER THIRTY-THREE

In the living room, the first thing he does is look for the roses, but they aren't on display like he'd imagined they would be, prominently in the center of the table, instead they're pushed to the far side of the piano that hasn't been touched since their daughter left. She hadn't wanted to bring it with her because the truth was, she admitted, she hated playing piano, she hated it her whole childhood.

His wife is in the kitchen. And he wonders why she isn't making a big fuss over thanking him: they had to have been too expensive, what was he thinking, doing that! But nothing like that! Nothing! Where is her happy dance, he thinks. His modesty? Why isn't she overcome with joy? Instead, she's bent over a pot, stirring.

"Noodle soup tonight." Does that sound all right to him? Today, she isn't feeling quite herself, that's why she went for something simple, it's quicker.

He has stuck his head through the curtain: everything is just like normal. On the counter, he sees sliced meat, four egg halves, a handful of bamboo sprouts. And he waits. And waits. Any moment now, she will turn around to face him. Laugh. Go, "Oh, the flowers." But she's brought the wooden spoon to her lips and is tasting the broth.

"A little too salty," she murmurs.

"A long day, was it?"

"Mm-hmm." She shoos away a fly.

Anything new? Anything unusual? he wants to add, but that would make it too easy for her. At any rate, she should arrive at the flowers on her own.

"Unusual?" She thinks for a second. "Why, yes!" Their daughter called earlier. She arrived safely. A short delay, one of the trains, an express train, had a technical problem, but it was resolved quickly. Thankfully. Otherwise, she would have missed her connection. "She says hello!"

"Anything else?"

He takes a step back. Takes his head out of the curtain. Something isn't right, he is becoming more and more sure the more he thinks it. Everything is just as it always is, but at the same time completely wrong. Maybe because the TV is off? He turns it on. They're recapping a soccer match. One player fell onto the field and didn't get up, his face contorted in pain, huddled in a little ball. They replay the scene. More commentary. A red circle marks the opponent's foul, which "as can be clearly seen here" never actually happened in the first place. Someone dives. The referee pulls a yellow card.

He clicks.

A historical drama. Blood gushing from a wound. Eyes staring feverishly up at the sky one last time, then—with the reflection of a bird inside—they roll back into the man's head. "He's gone," says a voice. A second voice begins to sob. The camera stays on the dead man, then switches to the bird flying away. Goes back to the dead man who, in the last second, when the bird was nearly out of view, manages a smile. The close-up shows the corners of his mouth curling up. "So young!"

He keeps clicking. And clicking. Images assemble before his eyes with the push of a button, then come apart again. How does it all work? He is clenching the remote; it is damp in his palm.

"Tastes good."

"Not too salty?"

"Just right." And he tells her about Itō and that he missed him, he set out first thing this morning for two weeks or maybe even longer, depending on how he feels, he's headed south, and he may well take a ferry from there and just keep going. "A real adventurer," he says.

"And his wife? What does she make of it?"

"She supports it, which means she must be a little worried, but she can't hold him back, nor does she want to. She said, 'What's the point?'"

"Well then. How nice for him." Her gaze drifts past him for a moment. She blinks. Looks down into her soup bowl.

"Nice?" And he refrains from asking her whether that's all she has to say about that.

"Yes, it's nice," she says. But she's lost in thought. Doesn't seem to be here at all, not here at the table, not in the room, seems to be somewhere else entirely.

"Did something happen?"

"No, what do you mean?"

And finally the thread breaks. Where did the flowers come

from, he wants to know, and he manages to remain calm in spite of how hurt he's feeling.

"Oh, those," she waves dismissively. One of her girlfriends brought them over for her, and she launches immediately into a story, as if she's been waiting to share it with him for the longest time, keeps talking like someone who has practiced what she was going to say numerous times in advance. "The friend from my dance class. You remember—Hiroko? I went to gymnastics with her a few times before? Whose husband—you remember, of course—the domestic violence? No?" Her cheeks are red, she's trembling. "Well, in any case, she came over for tea. Out of the blue. I was in the middle of doing laundry when all of a sudden I heard the doorbell. *Who could that be?* I wondered. Had she climbed all the way up the mountain, imagine that, just to wish me a happy birthday? Yes, today. My fifty-eighth. But it's all right that you forgot. Not important. We can make up for it later." Even the daughter had forgotten with everything going on. Completely understandable in her condition. And as for him, he shouldn't feel guilty about it, he knows she doesn't put much stock in her birthday anyway. "It's a day like any other; I'm just one year older. Hardly a reason to celebrate."

His head is swimming. But they are from me, he wants to say and point to the roses with his cane, the roses that looked so much more magnificent in the store than they do here among the books piled on top of the piano, a little scrubby.

He says, "That's nice of your friend to go out of her way to come all the way up here." Says this with a feeling of utter defeat. Because he considers it possible that his wife is telling the truth, and why couldn't she be? She could just as well have gotten them from Hiroko, a woman he's met once, but who apparently didn't leave enough of an impression for him to remember her. And maybe it's not her at all whom he's trying to remember, and the face that came to mind belongs to someone else? A black eye isn't evidence of anything after all.

And he pokes around, as they keep eating, in his separated pockets, he can feel the receipt between his fingers and how smooth it is. Later, when he is alone, he will take it out and have a good think. But for now. A sharp pain. It extends from his heart into his back, and from there hits the wall. His wife is standing up, her mouth hanging open. But what is she saying? He can't understand a single word. He sees her running to the phone. Then she returns.

Stay here with me, stay, he thinks.

"Shh," she says.

LATER

The daughter gave birth to a healthy baby boy. She sends them photos, almost daily, and he can hear him screaming in the background when she calls. She says it's because he's teething, which she can tell is happening because he's had diarrhea for days. She sounds a little tired. A little stressed. But when they ask her how she's doing, she replies, "Good." And that she has nothing to complain about, quite the opposite. There are babies who sleep a lot less, and nights are already quieter compared to even just a few weeks ago, when he wouldn't fall right back to sleep after nursing and she would have to carry him around until he closed his eyes.

She has a lot of back pain now from carrying him around all the time. Because the midwife was right after all: he was a big one. "He's going to be a sumo wrestler." She laughs. "You have to see his little legs!" No, the photos don't come close to what they're like in real life, and they should both come visit soon. As soon as he feels up to it, of course. Has he been resting? Yes? Now at least they have the stress of moving behind them. She heard from the brother that the new apartment is very bright and cheerful.

Sometimes he catches himself thinking some very sad thoughts. For instance, that life, his life, is only getting shorter and shorter. But then he tries to think of something else. Lifts the woodpecker on his desk. Watches him tapping away. That's less sad than he'd thought.

Unpack the suitcase. He put a check next to it. Its contents are now strewn across his desk, and he plans to clear it all off when he gets a chance. The suitcase itself is next to his bed. He's so used to it now that it would be a shame not to have it in the room. *Stop tripping over it :)* He crossed out the smiley face.

In the new apartment, which is directly next to the kindergarten—which looking back makes him happy now that he didn't have a third child after all—there are no pets allowed, so that eliminated the "dog issue" altogether. Sometimes, very rarely, as it turns out, he grieves for him, the white Pomeranian he would have bought if they had stayed up in the house, but the truth is he is relieved he doesn't have a dog; in his new role as a dog owner, he would not have been able to get used to talking with other owners about their dogs' excrements.

Shiro, he will admit, is in reality something he's held on to since childhood: His mother promised to get him a puppy when he started school, a promise she never kept. His father's response only added insult to injury, saying that if his mother hadn't died, she would surely have gotten him a dog. Why wouldn't his father give him one? His mother had been much nicer. His tears. His father's tears. And when he finally understood she wasn't coming back, he cried only because he understood, not because of the dog, and because his father kept repeating, "Don't cry," even though he couldn't stop crying himself.

His son spent a weekend helping them move, and when they

were all sitting down together one evening, he finally admitted he was on the brink of financial collapse. The fertility treatments cost him a fortune, and on top of that payments on the house they just bought, which he could see now was far too big for two people. Might they still have some money set aside? He and his wife wanted to give it one last try. He would pay them back, as soon as his head was above water again, and please, not a word to his wife, she didn't know anything about it.

At which point he patted him on the shoulder, a gesture that seemed to him fitting, because he had been wanting to do it for so long, pat his son on the shoulder, and he went against his doctor's orders and drank a beer with him that tasted just as he remembered, slightly bitter, slightly sweet, a little too warm.

"Life," he said, "is too short not to enjoy it." A sentence that sounded fake coming out of his mouth, but nobody noticed, both the son and his wife nodded in agreement. When he repeated it on the second beer, it sounded a little more real, and on the third—except they forbade him to do that.

His wife gave up her dancing. When asked why, she replied that there was no point in deluding herself. She is too old. And the instructor? She'd been wrong about him. A big mouth and nothing to show for it. And she is content, almost happy, that she can finally close this chapter. Some things just stay out of reach.

"Too bad."

He didn't try to convince her otherwise, and she was thankful for that.

"It's fine the way it is." What has been missed once cannot be made up for later, and accepting that as a fact is more elegant than wildly kicking at it.

Yes, it was with an almost dancer-like elegance that he agreed with her, because he felt sorry for her, and they left it at that, just like how they never returned to the subject of the roses, which of course had long since withered. He made a sincere effort not to go back to those. He's searched in vain for the receipt. His wife had taken the pants to the laundry with all the other clothes he was wearing at the time, and the receipt had probably been lost in the process. Or had she found it and drawn her own conclusions? Had perhaps one of the roses dried out and its petals kept in a box? These are the questions that occupy his mind, but not in a way that torments him.

From the new apartment they would not be able to see the annual fireworks display, which he sees as a great drawback, and he feels the agent should have put it in the description. He feels betrayed. A nice view, it said, and this is what they get! But it's still the same moon. The bunny in the moon keeps hitting the sticky rice.

He saw Chieko again. At least he thinks she was the one who squeezed past him into the elevator at the hospital he goes to regularly, once a month, for a checkup, which is why he and two others couldn't fit inside. But he caught her eye just before the door closed—she seemed to be asking him something. To this day, he wonders what it was. He doesn't have an answer for her.

A postcard from Fujimoto came just the other day. Not from Paris but from London, where the food might have been terrible, and the weather just all right, but the parks absolutely beautiful. The grass is so satisfying a color, he wrote, and it all goes back to the weather, so it comes full circle in the end. More on that when they next see each other. It would be too bad if they didn't.

And Mie? She never called. He's renewed his cell phone contract in case she does, and he often catches himself reaching for it when it hasn't even rung, catches himself playing golf on a dazzling green lawn while at the same time imagining what she would say to him: Maybe that it was worth it. Going back. Even if only for the mayonnaise on the okonomiyaki, she had three of them. And by the way. But with this, she only means to upset him.

Did he ever consider that everything could have been invented? Jordan and his mother. Chieko and her husband. The Terazawas. Everyone just a stand-in? And he the only real one, who had no idea about anything? Would that change anything? A mind game, wants to get under his skin. But he's deliberately playing dumb just to keep her on the line. Won't admit that he understands it's all fake. Swinging at golf balls. He just hit a hole in one. And he's never held a club in his life. He sees Mie's face in front of him. Through the window of the taxi, it looked darker than it actually was, and he asked the driver to roll it down—too late. He still remembers how she blew him a kiss, one of those gestures that only Mie was allowed. The taxi took a hard right, he leaned back in his seat.

"Beautiful, wasn't she?" he asked and began to explain the whole thing to the driver. But the driver only nodded in reply. They were silent the rest of the drive.

His wife was touched, when, as she was unpacking the moving boxes—what was she doing rummaging around in his things? That was his name written clearly on it, could she not read it?— the list of Paris flights fell into her hands. Had he wanted to surprise her? Yes, he'd been planning on doing just that. And he was touched himself when she, laughing, then crying, called him an "old secret-doer." If only she knew.

She didn't say more. Paged through the well-thumbed guide-book instead, laughing and crying at every line he had under-lined, at every dog-ear and every note scribbled in the margins. Since then, she has enrolled in a French course, and he hears her practicing her vocabulary as she cooks.

"Comment allez-vous? Je vais bien. Et vous?"

And it's nice to doze off to, like dozing off to soft, very soft music, which then tugs at his heart when he wakes up. So that he can feel: it is beating.

ACKNOWLEDGMENTS

I am grateful for everyone who waited so patiently with me. It was nice to be able to sit so long.

Special thanks to Thomas (you know why), Theodor (but how come?), my parents (one more time, because once isn't enough), Luise (for your encouragement), Hannes (for your questions), Stephan (for your laughter), Cristina and Sophia (*muchas gracias*), Koumoto Toyohiko (miss you), Anna (remember? At Wannsee?), Hans-Jürgen and Eveline (for so many moments together, at Brandstetter and elsewhere), Kris and Isabelle, Olivier and Françoise (thanks *je wel* and *merci*), Brigitte (keyword: Anpanman shoes), Hanako (for the piece of Japan you bring us each week), Erina (for the many words), Lisbeth (for coffee and cake), Frau Schlemmer (for the living room in winter), Anette (you had to wait the longest), and Theodor again (because I would like to tell you: for all of this. And because you smile like no one else can).